The Nixon Recession Caper

Ralph Maloney

The
Nixon Recession
Caper

W · W · NORTON & COMPANY · INC ·  *New York*

This book is for Liam,
who is tough.

Contents

The Nixon Recession Caper

I

Four Men of Substance

MISTER SANFORD CAMPBELL drove into a small, sad Amoco station in New Canaan, Connecticut, and stopped so that his gas tank was precisely before the regular pump. His car was a recent Pontiac station wagon he had had painted Silver Cloud by the Rolls people when new, in better times. A young attendant came from the dark of the garage to serve him, wiping his mired fingers on wool waste, in order not to soil the splendid fender. He put the nozzle in the gas tank and started forward with a wet squeegee in hand. "Yessir!" he called, alert to quality.

With an urgent smile, to avoid misunderstanding, Sandy thrust his grey-blond-handsome-distinguished head out the window and said, "Just a dollar's worth of the regular, please."

The squeegee stopped in the center of the windshield. Water coursed down crookedly. "A dollar's worth of the regular?" The boy's voice broke.

"Left my wallet at home," Sandy said engagingly.

"Okay." The attendant wiped at what he had spilled on the windshield and hurried to the pump. He ran it to one dollar, then banged everything back in place, disaffected. "One dollar," he said, offering his grimy palm.

Sandy put three quarters, two dimes, and a nickel into the hand. "Just out for a little drive, you know," he said.

The young man studied the change. "Okay, thanks," he said. Sandy started the car, gunned the engine, and raced out of the station, hoping somehow to convey that this was a madcap transaction and not an adult American male spending his last buck on gasoline. The attendant strutted cowboy-loose back into the garage to tell everybody about the sport in the Silver Cloud station wagon who just bought a dollar's worth of the regular, and paid with coins.

When he called his agent on the Coast, Harry Price always called when it was ten minutes to twelve in the East, because it was then ten minutes to nine in California, and the agent hadn't had time to organize his defenses, to remember yesterday's excuses. "Lew, listen," Harry said. "A little hedging, a little fudging I could take. There's a recession and everybody's entitled to steal a little. It shouldn't be, I'm Harry Price, not some Luigi-come-lately out of Cine Città, but I understand times are tough so I don't exactly demand every nickel that's coming to me. But this Allied-Universal you tied me into for the last picture, this guy Sid Kransky! He's picked up all the marbles and run! . . .

"Willya stop? That picture made a fortune at the nabes and the drives! And Kransky pocketed every penny! Every red fucking cent! . . .

"Never mind what Allied says the grosses were. You know better. You read *Variety*. When was *Variety* wrong about a gross? All right, a depression. Let Kransky share the depression with me. . . .

"Sue? How can I sue? It costs twenty thousand dollars just to run a survey, then there are lawyers to pay and I've got to live in the meantime and there's no money back here, either. . . .

"Do? I'll tell you what you can do! You had your hand in my pocket all these years, put your hand in your own pocket, come up with twenty grand to do a box-office survey, the major markets, and call Ron and tell him to donate his legal services. It's for a good cause, Harry Price. We can sue for half a million. Ron's been on my payroll for twenty years, tell him to get it up. The two of you put it together. We'll all make money. We can't miss. . . .

"All right. If you don't have any money, see if you can find some. Cash in your life insurance. Agents live forever anyway. Call me back today. No, today. Don't stall me and don't fake me out on the phone or I'll come out there and have your head. I'll be here all day. Call me. All right. I'll look to hear from you. Good-bye. Yes. I love you too. Good-bye."

Harry banged the instrument back on its cradle. He was at a desk, in his den, at home. He was surrounded by glossy photographs of himself with other greats. He took a dart from a cup on his desk and whipped it at a blown-up photo of Sidney Kransky, president of Allied-Universal Productions, who had gone south with the earnings from Harry Price's biggest picture. He hit big Sid on the nose. The dart sagged, but stuck.

Jack Carmody slept late these days in order not to wake thirsty before the liquor stores opened. He was lately bitter broke, and not only did he no longer have what is called a cellar, but he had taken to buying things like fifths, and even pints, and in consequence he drank the house dry every night. That was not the curse it first seemed, because drinking the house dry every night helped him sleep late mornings, until the liquor stores opened. All of him was awake but his eyes, which still wanted rest, but he forced himself to sit up on the edge of his bed. He lit a cigarette to wake his eyes, an Old Gold Filter King, a product he had introduced to America eighteen years earlier, to his own considerable enrichment. He stood, naked, a man who would have been called strapping in another era, and marched naked through the still house to the kitchen. The boys were away, in the Army and at college, and far from there being any servants, Mrs. Carmody had a small job. Naked he shook B-complex spansules from a jar into his mouth as a boy eats peanuts from a bag, and washed the spansules down with the best of a quart of cold grapefruit juice. As he felt the mess settle, Carmody thought, with satisfaction, *They want me dead, they're gonna have to take me out and shoot me.*

For the first time in his memory, Carmody was alone a lot now and, unaccustomed to silence, talked to himself—or rather addressed himself in a rhythmic profanity that mirrored his mind's workings. He walked up the hall to the bathroom, entered, and lifted the seat. "Take a whiz," he said, and did so. "Ah, the simple bloody pleasures of the poor." Before the bathroom mirror, he said, "Shave. No, shave after the bottles. Christ on a bike, you don't look like much, fucking swine, although what you expect with a quart a day at your age I don't know." He went to the bedroom, to the closet and the bureau. "Where are those Levi's the dizzy bitch bought me for my forty-fifth birthday? Levi's, for Chrissakes! Happy Birthday, Grandpa. Be a Marlboro man. Maybe she wanted me to go west and grow with the country. Here they are. Where are my fucking sneakers?"

Talking to himself in this way, Carmody dressed in work-type clothes and went to the kitchen again, where he drank coffee and read *The New York Times* until 10:45, which, to those who don't care about such things, is fifteen minutes before the liquor stores open.

Carmody went to the driveway and backed his station wagon firmly over a small garden and across the lawn to the bulkhead doors of the cellar. He slowly opened the tailgate of the car and then opened the bulkhead doors, also slowly, like a man embarked on a venture haste might damage. He climbed down the steps to the inner cellar door and opened it and crouched through the door and straightened, stunned and unbelieving. "The bottles!" he cried, looking about wildly. "My bottles! Where are my fucking bottles?" The cellar was empty but tidy, newly swept. "Where . . . ?" he began. He went to the inner cellar stairs and clambered up them with his hands as much as his feet, a beast possessed. In the kitchen he jerked the phone from its hook and dialed his wife's office. "Where are my bottles?" he howled at whoever answered. There was a pause and his wife's voice came on the line. "Mrs. Carmody," he said.

"Where are my fucking bottles!"

"Shhh. There might be somebody on the extension."

". . . bottles!" Carmody lost speech.

"I gave them to the Boy Scouts. They swept out the cellar for us."

"Three hundred beautiful green returnable Ballantine ale bottles? A year's work? Are you out of your bloody mind?"

"I'm going to hang up now," Mrs. Carmody said, and she did.

Carmody did not bother to hang up. He dropped the dreadful instrument on the counter and fell back moaning. "Fifteen dollars down there. Two quarts of scotch easy. She gave them to the fucking Boy Scouts." He found a chair and fell back panting.

But his mind regrouped, coalesced, counterattacked. He would shave, dress mature-casual, tone his cheekbones down ever so slightly with Mrs. Carmody's make-up, and go see Larry, the liquor store owner, and borrow a quart to get by on.

Mr. and Mrs. Samuel B. Deitsch were having what was for them an ugly marital spat, which is not to say they told one another vicious truths. They had been altogether intimate physically and mentally for twenty-one years, and such intimacy forbids truths. "Your brother Milton didn't go for midis because he couldn't afford to," Sam said. "So when midis couldn't make the

Thirty-fourth Street window at Macy's, where it's dark, Milton has a warehouse full of minis and he makes a fortune. That's brains?"

"I don't know who's brains in the family, but I know who's got money. Cash. Today. That's Milton."

"Milton? That line of his looks like rags made by children? Two years ago I took his mortgage."

"Hah! You don't even *have* a mortgage!" Joanna (Mrs. Samuel B.) Deitsch said. They were not at all practiced at quarreling, and threw lines like that around.

Stung by wild illogic, and indeed hit where he lived—Sam planned to take a mortgage to finance a new dress line in the fall —Sam retorted, "Milton's Judy she's got legs right up to her ass. Even if he could afford it he wouldn't go for midis, not with a wife built like Judy. God forgive me," he added. Joanna had been told by a boy when she was thirteen that she was built so close to the ground she'd need a rollerskate to get off a curbstone, and she had never forgotten it.

"If God gave me long legs I'd go blind looking at your bald spot. The glare," Joanna said.

Wounded again—remember these are inexpert fighters who don't take a blow well—Sam said, "Glare don't bother some people I know with long legs," and he could have plucked his tongue out on the spot. A truth was surfacing.

But Joanna's father was Seventh Avenue, and she knew about the models and fashion women, and accepted as her mother accepted. Rather than retort with a truth ("Long legs maybe but flat as a washboard. I've known about her for twelve years.") Joanna burst into tears. "Oh, Sam," she cried. "Go to Milton. He came to you when he needed help. . . ." She fell apart, like a prelim boy, from inexperience.

"Yeah, Milton." Sam sighed. "The thing is, when Milton came to me, I wasn't very nice to him."

"Well, next time you can be nice. There'll be a next time."

"You don't know. I lectured him an hour, hour and a half.

Didn't let him know I was going to write him a check until the very end." Sam sighed again. "I was a shit, Joanna. I'm sorry I was, and I know it's his turn now, but I can't take what I give and I'm not going to."

"I understand." Joanna had dropped crying as a tactic so abruptly that there were tears still on her jaw and no trace of moisture in her eyes. "Then let me go see my father."

"Better Milton. The lecture will be shorter and the check bigger."

"*I'll* go. He knows a bad year. We had plenty of them, growing up."

Sam got up from the kitchen table, where the ugly spat was being consummated. He put on a jacket. "Not your father. Last of all him. Starve first."

Exhausted by the unaccustomed quarreling and marshaling her reserves for a later attempt, Joanna asked simply, "Where are you going?"

"Out. Rob a bank. Knock over a candy store before I'll talk to your father."

Joanna smiled in a way that meant loving. "The kids won't be home till three-thirty." Perhaps that would solve things. It usually solved everything.

"I love you," Sam said. "I'm going out and drive around a while, think." He went out the door, and that was the end of the Deitsches' ugly marital spat.

2

The Bank & Two Clubs

MALCOLM HAYDEN was manager of the Vista Branch of the County Trust Company of Westchester, and Malcolm Hayden had nothing to do. Nobody—always ever nobody—came in for a loan or to make a big deposit. There was, of course, the A & P next door and the discount house a hundred yards away, and they were substantial depositors, but that was routine work and handled by the tellers. Hayden had nothing to do but wait for the phone to ring from the Katonah office and doodle on a pad. Once he had thought this the ideal employment circumstance, if you got paid on Friday, but he had married, four years earlier, an Arthur Murray dance instructress who had a waist so tiny that she came in two delicious pieces, and had not lost her figure one succulent whit in four years. When he had nothing to do but wait for the phone to ring and doodle, his wife came to him in fantasy, and his trousers became crowded and uncomfortable.

Managership of the Vista branch was a promotion and a great

opportunity for Hayden, on the raw face of it. But bank politics are as obscure as all politics, and after a week at Vista, Mal began to suspect that he had been put on a convenient siding to make way for the expresses, the younger men from better schools. As the meanest teller knew, the Vista shopping center, its bank included, was a carefully planned and bizarre error, rather like the Edsel. It had a supermarket, a superdeli, a superdrug and a great Willow Run of a discount house. Yet nobody came. Customers stayed away in the tens of thousands. Surveys had established beyond statistical doubt that a purchasing populace was nearby, yet boys raced minibikes and go-carts at noon on Saturday, the rush hour everywhere, in the empty parking lot. Nobody came. People did not know the shopping center was there, or they bought elsewhere, out of habit. Something had to be done, and quite soon, to bring the Vista shopping center to general attention, or they would all have to fold their tents, the bank included, and Hayden would be back at the number two desk in Katonah, or out looking for a job.

There was one strand of hope. It was more a longshot player's connivance than a hope, really, but Hayden took hope where he could find it. In the files he discovered that the Vista Plaza had been conceived, encouraged, instituted, planned, lobbied for, and financed by Thomas Clarke, at forty-two the boy wonder of suburban banking and now acting president of the County Trust Company. No boy wonder would want the Vista disaster on his record, and might indeed be very grateful to the man who redeemed Vista, put it on the map in big, black ink. Clarke knew who Hayden was, had given him the promotion personally. It was nothing to cash checks on, but it was a hope.

Hayden once again found nothing else to do, and he doodled a sailboat on his pad, the sail of which turned into a breast, and the memory of his wife assailed him to his great physical discomfort. Breasts and belly and bottom and thighs and smoothness and scent. AbbalaAbbalaAbbala. JesusGodJesusGodJesusGod. He crumpled the slip of paper before anybody saw it, and threw it into his wastepaper basket, hoping the janitor didn't smooth this sort of thing out, since he had as little to do as Mal Hayden, or possibly less.

Sandy Campbell drove his vast Silver Cloud vehicle into the empty, silent parking lot of the Vista Plaza. There was an acre of stores and not twenty cars before them. A siren sounded. Was it an air raid, in the name of God, and everybody run off to be with loved ones at the end? No. It was noon. Still the lot was moonscape and eerie. He pulled up before an A-frame building, the front wall of which was in glass, and which was proclaimed, on a small bronze plaque lower left, to be a bank. Sandy took his bill-fold from his inner jacket pocket, put his first unemployment check in the middle, and got out of the car. It would be embarrassing, but money is money, so carry it off. He lifted his chin, put a small, confident smile on his lips, and strode, manly but loose, into the bank.

Mal Hayden had doodled he knew not precisely what on his scratch pad, but there was a deep V in it, and he had shaded in the V warmly, with a hint of curls, before he realized he had a boy's erotic drawing before him. He crumpled the sheet and hurled it into the wastebasket. Looking up, he saw The Man coming through the glass door. Him. The Man who would somehow salvage the Vista Plaza and this insane branch of the County Trust Company, and Malcom Hayden's fortunes. The Man walked with his chin up, a small, confident smile on his lips, his stride loose but manly. He went to the receptionist's desk, and she led him to Hayden. They introduced themselves and shook hands. "Sit down, Mister Campbell," Hayden said.

Sandy sat. "As a general rule I bank in Westport," he said. "But this is sort of a different and delicate matter."

"I see."

"I don't have to tell you how bad business has been lately. . . ."

They exchanged rueful smiles. "And I have decided to collect what is coming to me in unemployment insurance."

"Nothing wrong with that." Hayden was shocked.

"Well, I've paid enough taxes in my time," Sandy insisted. He had no faith in his position, either. "But a lot of people down my way, Westport, might misunderstand, and my wife might learn about it, which would only worry her. . . . Anyway, I'd like to arrange to cash the unemployment checks here." Sandy opened his billfold and produced the check and spilled out credentials appropriate to a mutual fund vice president, which he had until recently been. He signed the check and Hayden initialed it, and they shook hands and Sandy went to a teller's window. Altogether an agreeable encounter.

Hayden was of course disappointed. But he had been around banks for fourteen years, and he knew a live one, an establishment winner, by sight. No drop-out loser ever had so many credit cards, and few losers had Greens Cards to the Southport Country Club, which Hayden had noted among Sandy's credentials. The Man, Him, was broke right now, but banker instinct told Hayden he was to be the savior of the Vista Plaza, and of Mal Hayden.

In a very different time—not so long ago, but before Franklin Roosevelt, of course—Southport Country Club boasted three eighteen-hole golf courses, two always in play and the third always at seed. But the blue-collar revolt of the Thirties spread the money (and little else) around more evenly, and wages and other operating costs rose. Taxes limited the amounts all but the very rich could afford for private golf and boating privileges. For all its grandeur, the Southport Country Club went broke, or close to it. Expanding the membership, taking in Irish and Italians—there had always been Jews—kept the deficit manageable until World War II, when the social fabric fell all to hell and everybody and his cousin moved to Fairfield County. With them came the land squeeze, and behind the squeeze the developers. It seemed silly to the old guard who ran the Club, and who were oriented toward the water, and sailing, anyway, to keep three golf courses, and so they sold the East course for a million and a quarter. The guard did its best to keep a straight face during the pillaging of the developer fool, but when the last of them had passed away, about 1967, the land alone was worth ten million, and the land and property some seventy million. In economic squeezes that followed, membership was expanded to include public relations people and Armenians and all kinds of careerist wogs, who immediately banded together with the Irish and Italians and excluded Jews. During the Eisenhower golf boom the Club went broke (or close) again, and the golf-oriented new guard sold off most of the waterfront property. However, in 1963 the deep fat fryer ignited and made a ruin of the kitchen and several ceilings, and faced with a large individual assessment, the membership voted to sell the West Course. The Club netted five million for the West Course, and survives on the money today. That left the Woodbury Course, site of the Woodbury Open and every twelve years the PGA tournament, the only course available.

Thus when we encounter the Southport Country Club in the next-to-last year of the Nixon Administration, we see a great, gracious rambling wooden building on top of a modest hill, its entrance facing north to the golf links and its terraces at the rear facing south toward Long Island Sound. There are tennis courts to the east, two in grass, and to the west a twelve-hole putting green where large sums are won and lost at cocktail hour on weekends. It is altogether a stylish place in an unstylish time, but a turn-of-the-century member returned would weep for the lost elegance. A snack bar does most of the food business, and the main kitchen staff has been reduced to three. Men drink bottled American beer at the walnut bars, watching professional golf on television. The swimming pool is a herringrun of children, all day every day in season. Scarcely anybody dresses for scarcely anything. Yet it is well to take a long look at the Southport Club today, because another revolution is upon us, and in twenty years if the Club stands at all, it will be a halfway house for addicts surrounded by another own-your-own-home slum.

As late as 1950, Southport members dressed and went to the Club for dinner twice and perhaps three times a week. Later it was used for small entertainments back and forth, the stewards doing the hostess's work. Later still it became a convenient place to meet for cocktails before going out to any of several excellent expensive restaurants that had grown up with Westport township. Through all change, however, Saturday night remained constant— or as constant as revolutionary times allow. Men and women and girls and boys dressed according to fashion, and well, and drank, and danced, also according to fashion, and not very well. Alcohol was commonly misused, especially around 1960, when the veterans of World War II seemed as one man to turn forty, and there were scandals galore then, too, for the same reason. Another change occurred about 1965, when marijuana was first smelled in the parking lot and on the terraces. By 1970, the fumes of pot and hash undeniably rose from some tables in the ballroom.

On a Saturday night in May, Brady (Iselin) Campbell and her husband Sandford entertained twelve friends at cocktails and dinner in the Haig Room of the Southport Country Club principally because Mr. Campbell could sign the bar and food check, and needed cash only for tipping. But that is running ahead of the story.

Fifteen men of every physical variety and three wispy women sat around a table large enough to skate on in the basement of Saint Michael's Episcopal Church in Southport. Each of the men and women had a cup of coffee, an ashtray, and a pack of cigarettes before him. A fat, brown man at the head of the table directed the conversation, which dealt with the uniquely human disease of alcoholism. The chairman had newspaper clippings and small pamphlets before him, which he used as points of departure for discussion. Jack Carmody sat near the foot of the table, listening to a man on his right pour out a tale of alcoholic loss and woe.

(It must be said here that Carmody was a man sharply impatient with himself, and therefore with the world, and in his impatience he heard what people were trying to say, rather than what they said. He overheard in his desire to comprehend and get on with things. This, then, is Carmody's version of what his neighbor said at the Alcoholics Anonymous meeting.)

"I diverted my trusting employer's mother by poisoning her puppy and stole the money from her purse that she had saved so her baby daughter could have an eye operation on her back. I went straight to Jimmy's for a couple of quick ones and next thing I knew I was in traction at Bellevue, playing with myself." The man lowered an enormous head by a very skinny neck to the table. There was silence.

"You have anything to tell us tonight, Jack?" the chairman said.

"I can't follow these acts," Carmody said. The horrors and tragedies of alcohol were not simply alien to him but quite beyond his comprehension.

"Well, you don't have to speak if you don't want to," the chairman said, "but you wouldn't be sitting here with us if you didn't think you had a drinking problem. We're here to help each other, and maybe we could all learn something from you. How do you think you became an alcoholic?"

"I'm not sure I am one," Carmody said. He paused. There was no sound. "That is a colossal therapeutic silence. My congratulations to all of you," he added drily. "Anyway. If I am an alcoholic, I didn't be*come* one, and I don't agree with a lot of you who think we were *born* alcoholics." He paused again. The rest maintained the elaborate silence. This was the first time Carmody had elected to speak since he started coming to meetings, and alcoholics are just as nosy as non-alcoholics, and they were dying to hear what he had to say.

"I didn't become an alcoholic, I was *made* one. *Hit*ler made me an alcoholic." Carmody paused again, and would just as soon have shut up, but the silence begged to be broken. "I was two hundred and eight straight days in the line going across Bavaria from wine cellar to wine cellar. Two hundred and eight days and I didn't draw a sober breath. I was nineteen years old."

Silence again. The chairman spoke, gently, to encourage Carmody. He was as nosy as the next. "Did you find that the brandy or the wine or whatever gave you courage?"

"I suppose," Carmody said. Long pause. "But that all evens out. You're braver at night but you're scared of your own shadow in the morning. . . .

"No. It was the cold. They have two seasons in Germany, August and winter. You could lie in a mudhole in October and have to chip ice from your feet in the morning. Everybody had pneumonia. Pneumonia and piles. So we drank everything that wasn't booby-trapped. Hitler made me an alcoholic." Carmody pushed back from the table. "*If* I am one. I'm not so sure. I know nobody called me an alcoholic until I went broke."

Broke. It was no longer war and fear and Hitler but broke, and familiar territory. The chairman urged Carmody along. "Did your being an alcoholic—if you are one, of course—have anything to do with your going broke?"

"I don't think so." Another pause, another rich silence. "Unless it was what you people call alcoholic unrealism."

"How would that be?" the chairman asked gently. Getting a new member to tell his story was harder than setting bones.

"Hah." Pause, silence. "For twenty years I hustled and connived to control the television advertising for the P. Lorillard Company. Twenty years, and I made it. And two years later the government outlawed cigarette commercials. Blooie. One Christmas I'm mayor of Madison Avenue, the next Christmas I'm a streetcorner Santa, ringing a bell."

"You worked for the Volunteers of America?" the chairman said. He had been a streetcorner Santa.

"No." Carmody shook his head in massive impatience. "No.

Just a figure of speech, for Chrissakes. I don't know where the Bowery is."

"I know where the Bowery is," the chairman said. It was a reproof. "A lot of us know where the Bowery is. Tell us. What do you think alcoholic unrealism had to do with your going broke? The cigarette thing was a government decision. You can't blame yourself for that."

Carmody stirred at the cigarettes, the ashtray, the coffee cup before him. "Simple as this," he said. "I knew about it. I saw it coming. I couldn't adjust. I just couldn't believe that you could work so hard so long for something and have it collapse under you. I became an overnight anachronism. What the hell, the client saw it coming and diversified. I should have started diversifying when I saw it all coming, but I started too late. By the time I tried to grab a soap account, a whisky account, this recession or depression —whatever you want to call it—was on us, and there weren't any accounts around to grab." He waved to dismiss. "Now let's get on with some real sad stories. I like to hear about you guys rolling in the gutter."

3

Life Styles

B ETSY C AMERON (Goetz, Hunter) Price had skin so pale and fair that one could almost see through her temples to the fretful turmoil inside her skull. Her hair was blonde and soft as a baby's in a breeze. Her mouth was a full, pretty thing which, pouted, could reduce strong men to swine. She was so small and delicately made as to seem ethereal, above sex, and in consequence she had been adored by scores of adult males who were still adolescents. At twenty-seven she looked eighteen and she would die looking eighteen. There was no part of her sturdy enough to bear the stamp of age. She looked like a child bride standing next to Harry Price, as she had looked like a child bride next to two earlier husbands, and a child mistress next to many other grown adolescents.

It is all a matter of life styles, really. Sam and Joanna Deitsch indulge in a little teasing and believe they are having a sordid quarrel; Harry and Betsy Price have a sordid quarrel and believe it

is conversation. Sandy Campbell staked his reputation and therefore his job that Dow-Jones would turn around and go back up at
800, but Dow-Jones went right on down to 600. Sandy is currently
making $43,500 a year less than he used to make, and is broke. On
residuals alone, Harry and Betsy make more than $43,500 a year,
but they, too, are broke.

Betsy lolled on a green chaise beside a rich but modest pool in
the scantiest of clothing. She was as tanned, all over, as her fair
skin permitted, so there was no purpose in her near-nudity but
nudity itself. Harry came along the pool from the house and sat
opposite her in a beach chair. He ran his fingers through his thick,
almost-white curls, the fingers trembling in frustration. "Splendid!"
he boomed. The "splendid" had been his trademark on the Harry
Price Theater in the early days of television. "Just bloody splendid!"

"Who's broke this time, honey?" Betsy asked.

"Our entire population west of the Continental Divide, apparently." Harry spoke to and on the East Coast differently from
the way he spoke to and on the West Coast. "New paupers being
made every day. My agent says he's penniless, my lawyer tries to
sell me apples. They both say they're broke. They say everybody on
the Coast is broke, living on residuals and unemployment. You
drop the name of a big star, they tell you he's broke, too. No
money!" Harry boomed. "Money!" echoed around the yard.

"What are we gonna dooo?" helpless Betsy cried, despairing.
She knew it shattered his manhood to be broke and was shattering
away.

"Don't tease. If I had twenty grand, twenty grand extra that my
wife or wives and their lawyers and Uncle Sam didn't know
about. . . ." Harry rose and paced and turned quickly to stare
keenly at Betsy. An actor is never offstage. "You don't have twenty
grand in a tin box somewhere, do you, baby?"

Betsy had money, but she was a Hollywood actress, and they
are good housekeepers, an old joke says. Let him keep the children

and you keep the house. "Let's move back to Puerto Rico, Harry. It's cheaper there, and I'm freezing here and it's the middle of May." She moved her hips on the chaise to get his mind off money, or to break the connection between her and money. She was tempted to help him.

"Oh, stop wiggling your fanny. You know I'm not much when there's money trouble. Look, Betsy." Harry sat again, and opened both hands to show candor. "You find twenty grand someplace, we have the accountants run a survey in ten or twelve major markets, and we sue. We can reasonably expect to get half a million bucks from Kransky. Then we can go to Puerto Rico, or Majorca for that matter, and you can work on your tan and we'll have a party."

Betsy was tempted. Harry was far and away her nicest husband. But she had made her money in a horrid jungle, and could not make herself surrender it to a man. To change the subject she put her hand between her legs and locked her thighs on it. "I don't have any tin box, Harry. Honestly." She rolled on her side, writhing on the chaise, her exquisite bottom pointed at Harry.

"Willya stop! You know I'm no good when I'm broke!"

"Oooo! Puerto Rico!" Betsy writhed on, quite deliberately teasing now. "The hot sun on my booah-die!"

"Lousy little broad," Harry said. The tableau was shattered by the arrival of a Filipino houseboy (yes, a Filipino houseboy) with two drinks on a tray. Betsy came blithely back from erotic transport and took a martini-rocks from the tray. She was about to flirt with Dudley, the houseboy, but Harry was pacing down the pool, too engrossed in money to notice. She ordered another martini by return trip and chicken sandwiches for lunch.

Like her husband, Helen Carmody talked to herself, but in her case it was because she talked always, and often there was nobody to talk at. She was driving her own car, a new Peugeot she had bought with money from her job, up a long driveway bordered by

stunted pines she had planted with her own hands to a large field-
stone and redwood house that had always been hers or had been
acquired by accident—at any rate a house that had long been
divorced in her mind from the man who had paid for it. She
parked between the family station wagon and the boys' jeep, and
taking up a package of groceries she had bought, she entered the
house by a side entrance she had had built and put the groceries on
an electric stove she had had installed three years earlier.

Her husband came into the kitchen and said mildly, "Hey." He
wanted only to discover which of the several people Helen Carmody was—mistress, old buddy, crazy lady—had arrived home
tonight. Helen said nothing, began unpacking the groceries furiously. "Now what in hell is the matter?" Carmody asked mildly.
The luck of the psychic draw had brought home tonight the Crazy
Lady. He went to the freezer and put fresh ice cubes in his glass
and poured whisky on top of them.

"Where did that come from?" Helen demanded.

"The liquor store."

"You know what I mean!" Helen turned furiously to face him.
"You're supposed to be in AA, the mortgage isn't paid, I buy
groceries or we'd starve to death. There's hardly any gas in the car,
the television set is broken . . ." Here Carmody's impatient inner
ear took over again, and he heard, roughly, "Do you think I like
driving nine hundred miles round trip seven days a week to be
chained next to a mule driving a millstone and whipped when I
falter just so we can remain in this hideous crumbling cavern given
me by mother? Only to come home at night to force gruel through
the trembling lips of a has-been lush? Do you think I like that?"

Carmody put a touch of water from the tap over his whisky.
"Yes," he said, for it was true. He was not an especially taciturn
man, but when his wife was being the Crazy Lady he remained
largely silent, as he would not sing along if Caruso were singing.

"Jeeziz!" Helen said, whirling to slam canned goods into cup-
boards. "Twenty-four years married to a drunken sex maniac who

was never home to watch his boys grow up, lushing at 21 with every office floozie on Madison Avenue . . ." Carmody, as noted, overheard. He took his drink down the hall to the bedroom, where he dressed with automatic meticulous care in the uniform of a Lieutenant Colonel of the National Guard. Through two shut doors and fifty feet away, Helen could still be heard hissing great curses and banging pots. The Crazy Lady.

Pinning on his jewelry of rank, Carmody slid into a dream that was of recent manufacture but was daily gaining power and clarity. First he got about ten grand ahead, then he took a small apartment in the City and got some two- or three-hundred-dollar-a-week job —in Production or Traffic, a job without the pressure of account work—and he had lunch with friends every day and drinks with friends at night, and there would be women. He had always been lucky with women. Why the hell had he married a girl he didn't like? Who didn't like him?

Press on with the dream. Young Jack is married, in the Army, and has a wife and kid in Germany. He can take care of himself. Bobby plays football at Delaware. They take pretty good care of him. Pay off the house. Leave it to the boys. God knows what it will be worth in twenty years. Or leave it to her first, then to the boys? No. By all means outlive her. (Offstage, Helen cried, "God-*damn* this miserable old refrigerator!" Crash-O! went the door.) If he remarried, as part of his fantasy, he would marry a friend.

When he was dressed, Carmody went back to the kitchen to fix his drink. Helen was on the phone, gabbing amiably about nothing at all with her friend Ellen. She lifted her drink, toasted him over the rim of her glass, and chatted on with Ellen. Carmody poured only a very little whisky over the wasted cubes in his glass—he liked a little alcoholic help for his Guard meetings, but was exceedingly wary of too much help—and he wondered just which person his wife was now, mistress or old buddy.

Helen hung up and smiled at him. "You look very handsome in that uniform," she said. "Can't we have just a small war, like with

Mexico, so you can wear your uniform all the time?" She added whisky generously to her drink. "Thirty-five-cent martinis at the Officers' Club, Saturday night dances. That was a time."

Helen was being his old war buddy now. "I wish they'd have a small war, too. I could use the job."

"Oh, don't worry about it," Helen said. "We'll get by."

Carmody went out the door. The dream of an apartment in the City and drinks with friends, and women, diminished, but it would return in force when he was once again confronted with the Crazy Lady.

Lisa Deitsch was in every respect an accident of birth. Earliest on, she had been an unwanted pregnancy. Sam and Joanna already had a boy and two girls, and figured they had done their population bit. But Joanna really didn't want an abortion, and they decided whatthehell we both like kids, let's have another boy. So Lisa came and she was all girl and Sam and Joanna were overjoyed, of course, except that they weren't overjoyed.

But Lisa made her own joy. She was a quiet, happy affectionate baby, but more important, by the time Lisa was two, the Deitsches were compelled to recognize that against all genetic probability, their mating had produced a genuine beauty. Her face and figure were like a composite picture by a gifted artist of every element of beauty discernible in the two negligible bloodlines. Both sides of the family claimed her at once and avidly. "Look. Audrey's eyes," they said. "Audrey's eyes. Look."

The Deitsches' family room was the playroom downstairs. Upstairs, both floors, was spare and Yankee, fashionably Westport, with harsh chairs and wooden eagles. Downstairs was dark and close and rich, deeply carpeted, with dark leather armchairs to get lost in. The lighting was subdued and in many colors. Tribal tastes do not abandon six thousand years of the Levant for a generation or two in Hungary and a cup of coffee in New England.

When the Deitsches were away, and they thought of home, they thought inevitably of the basement room.

Sam Deitsch sat in a synthetic fur sling chair holding, under a cone of white light, the Real Estate License Exam Handbook. Lisa came down the stairs, sockless in loafers, wearing harlequin corduroy wash'n'wears and a frilled white blouse. She launched herself at Sam and sat all unconscious and quite hard on the side of his lap tailors would say he was "dressed" on, crushing and pleasuring him. She put her arms around Daddy's neck and kissed him fragrantly and said, "Read to me." Lisa was eight.

"You don't want to hear this, honey," Sam said. (Is that a bosom she's growing already? Can't be.) "It's dull old real estate talk. Daddy's studying to be a broker." (He's not broke enough.)

"Read to me anyway."

Anything. "Seventy. Must an agreement be recorded? No, but it is permitted by statute if the agreement is acknowledged by the parties, or one of them. And, the same law applies—"

"I love parties," Lisa said.

"And I love you." Sam kissed the incredible cheek. "You're the prettiest thing ever happened to the state of Connecticut."

"I know," Lisa said, agreeably.

"Let Daddy study now, Lisa," Joanna said. She coughed, as one does when encountering a love scene, and walked evenly down the stairs to indicate mission and purpose. "There's Yodels and milk upstairs. You love Yodels."

"Oh, good." Lisa said. She dismounted Daddy with (what had to be) an unconscious backhand chop at his jewelry, kissed Mommy on the cheek, and went up the stairs. Sam and Joanna did not speak for the best part of a minute, savoring the delicious absence. Sam broke the silence because he was beginning, just beginning, to learn that he was jealous of Joanna for her share in Lisa. He did not want to learn that, so he gave Joanna the examination book. "Go ahead. Ask me," he said.

Joanna rummaged in a catechism sort of section at the rear of the book. "Can a written agreement be varied or modified orally?"

"No," Sam said angrily, as though it were fight talk. "No verbal agreement between the parties to an agreement are admissible to vary its terms or affect its construction."

Sam had his hand over his eyes. (Oh, my God. He's not crying, is he? What will I do if he starts crying?) "You're really very good," Joanna said. "You could take the test tomorrow. With your contacts you should make a fortune." (Oh, thank God he's not crying. Just tired.) "What if there is a defect known to both parties before the agreement is signed?" Joanna asked, from the book.

"What if, what if," Sam said. "What if I had tits I could be your grandmother."

"Sam. Come on."

"I make dresses, garments for ladies, clothes. I don't screw young couples need a house, shelter."

(Was he going to cry now? Don't look.) "Sam. You can put out a new line in the fall. Everybody will help. But until then, what harm is there in a real estate broker's license? My father made his big money in real estate, and he was Seventh Avenue."

"Okay," Sam said. "All right. What if? What if? Let me hear the question again."

Brady Iselin Campbell had a serenity that put the world in awe of her. The serenity derived from a very simple accident of personality. Brady did not think of sex unless she were in bed, any more than she would think of driving unless she were in an automobile.

The rest of us, stewing in our carnal juices all day and half the night, say, Of course she thought of sex when she wasn't in bed. Keyholes and great phallic cucumbers and horseback riding and the flash of electric muscle or dark body hair, and the sudden assault of strong smells or rhythmic sounds. Of course she thought of sex.

But she didn't. Not Brady. Not until she was in bed with her husband, when it was time to think sex, and Brady could be as devious as Tammany and as involved as a civil proceeding. Between such encounters, however, the demon sex didn't strike her. This gave Brady an evenness and a directness in dealing with an uneven and indirect world that earned her considerable awe, and few friends. She didn't need friends. She treated everybody well and everybody treated her with respect, which is what a sane adult should ask of the world, although we all ask more. There are tragically few sane adults around, perhaps because it doesn't sound like much fun.

If you are sane to begin with, however, sanity is not the beastly chore it seems at a distance, and Brady Campbell enjoyed the genuine admiration of her competitors in the housewife-and-mother dodge, a considerable attainment, and she had her children's love, and was treated by her husband with a certain ardent reverence that brought his best manners to the simplest exchanges. And all this extraordinary, lucky lady had, at root, was an inability to consider sex unless she were involved in loving. Seems simple enough. It's not.

Sandy fondling reached in the night, traced the flare of hip, and pulled Brady's bottom to his lap. She folded to him, then stiffened. "What's the matter, love?" Sandy said.

"I don't know why I bring it up now." Brady rolled away and up on one elbow. "But I could use some cash."

"I know how you can make a fast ten bucks."

"All right. Later. But I've been playing golf with Joanna and I owe her about forty dollars."

That was the end of loving for a time. "Joanna! Deitsch?" Sandy said. "You can beat Joanna's brains in."

"I know. But I haven't been. I think really, I really think, really. . . ."

"Yes."

"I think she needs the money. I think she's playing for the

money. So I give her every break, you know?"

"I know, honey. But we're not so well off either, right now. These are tough times for everybody, and especially us, tell you the truth."

Brady got up, to be out of bed until money things were set straight. "Well, I kind of need forty dollars cash. Joanna hinted she could use it."

"You need cash, I'll get it for you," Sandy said bravely. "Come back to bed."

"I'm going to the john a minute," Brady said. "Where will you get it?" She left the room without waiting for his answer. It was enough for her that Sandy said he'd get cash for her.

"Don't worry about it," Sandy said to the ceiling of the empty bedroom. He knew a place where there was a lot of cash. It would not come to mind exactly then, but it was there, somewhere in his mind, and he would think of it.

4

The Posted List

THE HAIG ROOM at Southport Country Club was more like the living room of a great home than a private dining room. There was a huge fireplace center, before which a small busy bar was now operating, and a vast round table left, set for twelve. The Haig Room was named for Walter Hagen, and his feats were commemorated on a plaque right of the double doors. The room seems a gracious gesture to the memory of the great Hagen, but its origins were less than gracious. In 1925, the Professional Golfers Association Tournament was played on the Woodbury Course, but pro golfers were not permitted use of Club facilities. Walter Hagen, PGA champion in '24, '25, '26, and '27, not to mention 1921, announced he would not compete unless the Club was opened to professionals and indeed until he was given a room of his own to entertain in. The Board met hastily, and the president, a man grandly named Hillary Allerdice, said, "If he must have a room, let's give him this one. We only use it twice a year anyway."

Thus the Board Room became the Haig Room, and the details of the transaction lost in time, Southport members today congratulate themselves on the group good taste that established this memorial to the unforgettable Walter.

As host, Sandy Campbell was standing near the doors, before the plaque celebrating Hagen. He and Cal and Bitsy Magruder and Dwight and Elaine Carleton were reviewing private school and college tuition costs with the moderate outrage of people who could afford it all anyhow. The talk of thousands of dollars annually being eaten alive by headmasters at Choate and Yale brought to Sandy a sudden and wildly discomforting realization: He had not paid his dues or bar tick in many months. He might perhaps just have to pay for this preposterous party, and with a very doubtful check. Sandy excused himself and crossed the huge old lobby, dark boards a foot wide, newly waxed, chairs strewn at random, unoccupied. The practice of posting delinquent members had been revived for the first time since Truman, and it had occurred to Sandy that he might just possibly be posted. The bulletin board was at the right of the dining room-ballroom, and in its upper right corner was a separate framed space with two lists typed on crisp letterhead stationery. One list was for those far behind in dues, and the other for those far behind in dues and bar tick. Sandy stopped before the bulletin board and pretended to be deeply interested in the notices, then looked sharply up at the posted lists. He was not on either. He could sign for this stupid party, and just tip in cash. He sighed in great immediate relief. And for reasons that only became clear much later, he tore the right-hand posted list (dues *and* bar tab) from its pin and put it in his inner dinner jacket pocket. He went back to his guests.

Harry Price no longer saw a movie when he watched a motion picture. He watched money unfolding. If, for tragic example, the Mimi of the melodrama took her life in unutterable dismay by jumping from a bridge, Harry did not think, "How sad. Pretty girl drowning herself over one teensy pregnancy and a bad set of lungs." Instead Harry thought, "Location. Must have taken three days to set up that shot. Boom camera. Long shots. Zoomers. Tank shots. I would have had her slash her wrists in the bathtub. Dozen close-ups. Shoot it all in one morning. Save thirty grand." The Prices were watching the end of an in-flight movie on a New York to Los Angeles flight. "Is Raquel Welch *really* a dyke?" Betsy said.

"Shush," Harry said impatiently. The most exciting part of the movie, the credit crawl, was on the screen.

"As long as we had to go first class we might as well drink up the difference," Betsy said. "Ring for the stewardess."

"Shush!" The names of people Harry knew, had worked with, admired, hated, used, been cheated by, had borrowed from and loaned to, were on the screen. For example, his friend Jamie Gorshin was Art Director, and Harry thought, good old Jamie. Got to use him next time if he's still speaking to me.

"Never mind," Betsy said crossly. "I'll ring for the stewardess." She reached up and pressed a button.

Harry sat back. "Dick Hines did the score. We have to use him on the next picture. He plays the piano beautifully and knows a million old songs."

The stewardess arrived. "Yes, sir," she said.

"A martini and a scotch and water," Betsy said.

"I don't want a drink," said Harry.

"Two martinis then," Betsy said.

"It's ten minutes to ten," the stewardess said, looking at her watch archly.

"What are you, Big Ben?" Betsy said. "Two martinis, please, rocks." The stewardess left without a word.

"This isn't like the flight to Rome, you know," Harry said. "We have to pay for these drinks."

"Then why did we go first class? We could have gone in the same airplane and saved two hundred dollars."

"Harry Price get off the back of a plane? Are you crazy?"

"Well, for two hundred bucks, Betsy Cameron will get off the back of the plane, and I'm paying for this trip."

"Stop it. They find out we're broke out here, I'm dead and so are you."

The stewardess appeared with a two-ounce Heublein's martini-mix bottle and a two-ounce bottle of Gordon's gin. She poured them together over ice in a large plastic cup. "Oh, that's *just* how I like them," Betsy said, greatly pleased. "How did you know?"

"You're in our flight book, Miss Cameron," the stewardess said. She accepted money from Harry and left.

"See?" Harry said. "Everybody knows who you are. You fly tourist and that girl tells her boyfriend, who tells his agent, and everybody knows we're broke, and on the Coast that means we're dead."

Betsy dropped a hand idly into Harry's lap and squeezed. She felt intolerably good about being recognized. "Well, we're not broke. I've got ten thousand waiting in Los Angeles and you can get ten thousand someplace, and we'll sue Sid Kransky and be rich kids again."

"I just can't thank you enough for coming up with some cash, Bets. I know we can beat this thing. I can feel my confidence coming back."

"So can I." Betsy said, with another small squeeze.

Ten names. Ten men of substance and accomplishments whose names were on public display for nonpayment of bills, bills that for some of them would have been truly negligible in better times. What difference would Club dues and bar tick have made to Jack Carmody, to name one, when he hired and fired a half-dozen situation comedies a year in the name of Old Golds? On the other hand, Cal Magruder was listed, and Cal, while not at all stupid, did not know how much money he had. It was either a hundred sixty-seven or a hundred seventy-six million. Bunny Hibbard was on the list, but he had married unspeakable money, and every so often Lorraine shut him off, at least financially. She would write the Club a check now that she had embarrassed Bunny. Two of the men on the list were out of the country, and one of them had a temper problem and would lift the roof off the Club three inches when he came home and discovered he had been posted. Another was a man named Baker, celebrated for his thrift, who probably would not pay without being posted, but was far from broke.

That left five names. One was Conrad Hansen. Connie and Sandy had gone to St. George's and Dartmouth together. Well, one way to find out. Sandy got on the wall phone in the kitchen and dialed Connie Hansen. They talked small for a while, then Sandy said, "Things as tight with you as the rest of us?"

"Tighter."

"I really could use (What's a good figure?) a thousand dollars. Can you help me out?"

"I guess so, Sandy. Yes. Sure. Can you come by?"

"I'm waiting for the mail. Got some checks in it, I hope. I'll come by after lunch."

"Come by earlier. I'll buy lunch."

"Thanks, Connie. Next week some time. But I'll see you this afternoon." They rang off. Sandy went back to the breakfast nook and crossed Hansen's name off the list. He also discovered he had solved his petty cash problem for some weeks to come.

Four names left. Jack Carmody, Sam Deitsch, Harry Price and Doug Hamilton. Sandy went to the kitchen wall phone again and called Hamilton. "Doug," he said. "I've got an offer for seven thousand on the property out back. I told them I had to call you first."

"Sandy, I offered you five thousand cash in hand for that property. The offer still stands. If you can get seven thousand cash, grab it."

"Okay, Doug. I'll call you back. I'll let you know." Sandy hung up and crossed Hamilton's name from the list. He wasn't broke.

He wasn't very nice, either. The property was worth at least twenty thousand in better times, and Doug had offered five for it when he knew Sandy was scratching to make ends meet.

That left three names. Carmody, Deitsch, and Price. There was no point in calling them because it was common knowledge they were all three broke right now. Besides, Sandy didn't know them well enough to call them up on a Saturday morning and start asking questions.

Three. But three men for what? What on earth did he need three penniless executives for? It was still not clear, or not articulated. But it was in his head, and would come to the fore sooner or later.

Sandy put on a jacket and went out the kitchen door and walked down the driveway to the mailbox. Three male poodles, representing three generations, gamboled and sniffed and examined the driveway about and before him. There was all kinds of second class matter in his mail, addressed to "Resident." There was also an unemployment check, which Sandy put quickly in his pocket. Walking back up the drive amid the three generations of poodles, he decided the first thing Monday morning he would drive over to Vista and cash the check at the silly little isolated bank he had discovered. And he realized, then and only then, that the Vista bank was the secret place in the back of his mind where there was plenty of cash, that the Vista bank was why he had taken the posted list, that the Vista bank was why he needed Carmody and Deitsch and Price. After a first chill of fright, he saw the entire reasonableness of the project, and discovered that all unaware he had thought out a robbery. That plans had already been formed in the dim reaches of his mind, and needed now only to be put into effect.

Jean Hayden bathed while her husband was at work. She could not get out of the shower in one piece, a private pun, if he were around the house. If he would just once say No, thank you, or

I'm tired, or I have gas. Anything. Then she might be some kind of decent wife to him. But all she had to do was bend over the sink and Whoopee! she was mounted. It had come to this: Drying herself before the big mirror on the back of the bathroom door, she did not posture, did not even examine herself, and kept the towel between her body and the mirror, lest the naked image somehow be imprinted on the mirror and send Malcolm careening around the house in a spasm of lust.

When they were first married they seemed, and in fact were, evenly matched. But Mal had the persistence of an artist, and he never said No. Not once in four years of marriage. She was at first dismayed but game, then apprehensive, and lately frankly nervous, too nervous for any kind of joy. And it was not her fault, dammit. If he would say No once, then she could coax and tease him and get turned on herself. But he had never, not one time, indicated reserve or restraint. Even when his leg was broken and he had a cast from toe to hip. No need to make eyes at Old Faithful.

Jean put on slacks and a blouse and made her daily tour of the house. She pretended to be looking for something, but was really only pleasuring herself in her surroundings. The house was the first thing in her life that she had wanted badly that had not been a disappointment when she got it. Everything else—high school, driver's license, college, and especially marriage—had been a cheat, but not the house. Touring it she frequently hugged herself, as one does in the cold. If there was a drawback, it was the marriage that had brought her the house. Weary to the bone of Mal's unwearying desires, she had shut him off, blaming him for the old house in Katonah. Mal's lust conquered his banker's prudence, and he went deeply into debt to buy a small palace in Westport. And now she, Jean, had her house, and was expected to consort with Mal continually. It was an exhausting bore to please him, and she felt inadequate in the face of his great pleasure, and unwomanly, and nervous.

She stacked the dishes in the washer. Altogether, the three or four months she had been on strike had been the happiest of their marriage, except for the first year, of course. Perhaps if she thought of something else to strike for, she could shut him off again and get some sleep. A new car? No. That was being silly and spoiled. She had a Volks and she only used it for shopping and it was fine. Something about Westport, then. They weren't part of the community at all, and knew scarcely anybody. Yes. Something in around there. Let me see. Yes. Why can't we join the Country Club? Southport, it was. And meet the people around here who *are* somebody, who *do* things. Don't touch me, Malcolm, I'm . . . What am I? I'm in mourning for Martin Luther King? No. We never go out and see anybody. We don't know anybody here. (I don't feel like it.) Why can't we join that Club? We have a house and you're with the bank. It's not as if you sold used cars or something. Don't we know anybody who's a member? Who could put us up? Let go, Mal, please. I don't feel well.

Carmody had a sweet lie, the ball nesting in a patch of Bermuda bent where the green had been ten years ago. He scrubbed the face of his sand wedge idly, relishing the shot. He had played indifferently all morning, not wanting to scare Sinclair back to his own league, but now it was time to put away his toys and put some meat on the table. He bent his knees slightly, locked his head down and (Carmody's phrase) cold as a tear on a Laplander's tool hit through the ball with a satisfying crunch of turf. He did not lift his eyes until the ball was so high it could not be seen unless you knew exactly where to look, and Carmody knew exactly where to look. It took the wind, very high, and came left, and dropped almost gently on the green, where the spin took and it rolled back to the pin, leaving a two-foot putt.

"Great shot, Jack!" said Sinclair. They got into the golf cart and drove toward the green. "You taught that wedge to talk yet?"

"A little French," Carmody allowed. Pity. Jim Sinclair was a nice enough sort, and Carmody could teach him a lot about this stupid game, but Sinclair's grandfather had made intolerable money and Carmody needed meat for the table, and that was the end of pity.

Jack putted out crisply—there was no time for nonsense now— and held the flag for Sinclair, who was thirty-five or forty feet away. After a great deal of waggling, Sinclair attacked the putt, as inexperienced golfers will do, and damned near holed out. But the ball rimmed and hopped and rolled six-seven feet downhill. Carmody stepped away with the flag as Sinclair set to putt again. Sinclair waggled his putter and fretted, and as he made his stroke he bit down on a bad tooth, as they say in the game, and came up two feet short. He looked up at Carmody.

"I wouldn't give that putt to my own son," Carmody said with a short laugh. He had conceded longer putts all morning. "Play it out."

"Okay, Jack," Sinclair said loudly, to get his nerves back in order. He concentrated and hit the ball exactly right, and the ball hit something else exactly right—a blade of grass, a worm's tail— and stopped left. He was so furious at fate he almost missed the final tap. He was now blown sky high, and he knew it, and Carmody knew it.

They got into the golf cart. "Were you playing here when they still had the west course?" Carmody asked pleasantly.

"No." Sinclair's open blond face was blue with funk. He dreaded the eighteenth. While he was not a Carmody-caliber drinker, he wished he had a flask along.

Carmody missed an eagle on the eighteenth by a maiden's hair. Sinclair drove well, but his irons turned to porridge and his putter became a cattle prod and he took a nine.

"You would have liked the west course," Carmody said, accepting money. "It favored your kind of game."

"Just what the hell does that mean?" Sinclair demanded. He had known all along he was playing over his head, but was just beginning to suspect he had been hustled.

"Well," Carmody said, laughing cheerfully in the blue-blond face. "For one thing it only had sixteen holes, and you play great golf for sixteen holes." He laughed again.

Sinclair laughed genuinely, and his face lost its horrid blue. "Sonofabitch, Jack," he said. "You just took candy from a baby."

"Sixty bucks," Carmody said, making it a trifle. "You can afford it. Come on. I'll buy drinks and lunch." They returned the golf cart to the shed, and hefted the big leather bags up to the Club. They went into the Back Nine bar and ordered drinks and sandwiches. Carmody paid. Meat for the table.

5

A Business Lunch

AFTER ONE HAS seen his father drunk, he never sees the same man again. Once Sandy Campbell learned the Vista bank was to be his source of ready cash, he no longer saw it as a bank. A bank was a big marble edifice in Westport where he talked mortgages and car loans with friends. The isolated A-frame building in Vista was not a bank but a target he had selected and a problem he had to solve.

He drove across the ludicrously empty parking lot and stopped before the bank, just as he had a week earlier. But this time his mind was full of entrances and exits and back roads and the distances to highways. Entering the bank he smiled at the tellers, but he counted them, too. Three women under thirty. The guard was a stringy old veteran who might have played the Spirit of Deathly Boredom in a pageant. The gun at his hip pulled his body sideways. The only physically fit male present was the manager, Hayden Something or Something Hayden, who was a lightweight, and would be no trouble at all.

Sandy reintroduced himself to Hayden and got his initials on the back of the unemployment check. The meeting was not so cordial as the first because Sandy was preoccupied and seemed aloof. Hayden took this to be a slight snub, and was delighted. If Campbell was really The Man, the class and money to salvage Vista and Mal Hayden, naturally he'd snub the young manager of an abandoned bank branch. Sandy accepted money from a teller, whom he was even then gauging for boldness or caution. She counted the money three times before handing it to him, and he decided she would be most cautious in the face of danger. In the car, he wrote the speedometer mileage on an envelope to clock the miles from the bank to his home. By far the larger portion of his mind howled that it was all an insanity, but a smaller section, energized by his real need for cash, said that even an insanity should be planned with some care, that there was no earthly reason *not* to know the mileage between the bank and his home, or how many tellers, guards, and managers were in the bank on a given Monday morning. It also reminded him that the more you know about an adventure, the less adventuresome it becomes.

His first thought, for while he was not a lazy man he had lost the habit of action in his recent idleness, was to walk into some strange bank with a paper bag and present a note to the teller saying *Fill this bag with ten thousand dollars or I will* . . . Will what? And that was the end of the thought. He also felt without special vanity that he was too conspicuous a person to escape unidentified. Tall man, blond, graying, tanned, quite (no vanity here, either) handsome. Looked very much like a man named Campbell who lives down in Westport. Then his fantasy took the sordid form of policemen visiting at twilight, when the family was at dinner. The walk into a bank with a note and a paper bag simply collapsed of its consequences.

But the bold stroke. Armed, disguised (stockings or something), loud, vigorous. Hit them and clean them out before they knew what was going on. That appealed to his imagination, his almost-dormant sense of adventure, and, strangely, his good sense. It was, on reflection, not so horrid a piece of folly after all.

The mechanics of a bank robbery had been worked out in the back of his mind before Sandy had any idea he was to engineer such a robbery. It was an operation for four men, three armed and a driver. One man covered the door, the other two covered the tellers and took the money. The driver, Sanford Campbell of course, stayed outside with the motor running.

But for the hundredth time the whole plot exploded into a welter of obstacles and perils—specifically, guns and prison. He dismissed the bank robbery as adolescent speculation and weaving of the wind. He still had shares of The Bank Street Fund, his old firm. There was some IBM his father had left him. He owned two acres of Westport land, zoned and ready for building, right in his own back yard. He would sell the stocks short and sell the land at a quarter of its value before he drove up to a bank and let three armed men out of his car.

However, at the thought of selling short and being gypped on his land, Sandy's teeth ceased to mesh properly. They were set, literally, on edge and, again literally, hurt him. For the hundred-and-first time he reopened in his mind the robbery of the bank at Vista.

98.7, Sam Deitsch's score on the Connecticut Real Estate License Board examination, was the highest recorded since the War, and could reasonably be considered the highest recorded ever, since the pre-War test was a joke. Armed with his license and a certain modest confidence due to his high test score, Sam made an arrangement with Doug Hamilton of High Ridge Realty. After a week of sitting religiously still in his office, Sam complained to Hamilton not so much of inaction as futility. Hamilton then pushed some hopeless cases and lost causes toward Sam and Sam pursued them all with great energy and, to Hamilton, alarming tenacity. At length he actually sold one of the houses, a forty-two-five that wasn't worth thirty-five, and arranged the mortgage and passed the papers and made himself eight hundred dollars after the commission had been split and expenses deducted.

With a nicer man, such success would have been rewarded with a few of the better prospects to come into the office, but Hamilton was a businessman, not a nice man, and he reckoned that if Sam could make money where he, Hamilton, couldn't see any, then *give* him all of the hopeless cases. He did, and Sam made no more miraculous sales. He showed houses to people he knew were shopping for fun, and he showed fifty-thousand-dollar houses to couples who drove up in ruined Fords. He arranged a couple of rentals, so there was some money coming in, and all the time he told himself he was learning, and not wasting his time. He refused to be discouraged.

One Saturday morning, Doug Hamilton ushered into Sam's office a burly bearded man with a boy at his side. The boy had a great round head and seemed especially timid. The man sat down hugely and looked around Sam's office, estimating its status. "Guess your boss didn't figure me for a live one," he said. "I don't blame him. No woman with us and it's the woman buys the house, I suppose."

"Mr. Hamilton regularly turns more than half his clients over to me," Sam said.

"And makes money on the rest." The man laughed. "My name's Thompson, Jim Thompson." He gestured at the boy. "We're from Seattle. The woman is dead, if that sets your mind to rest."

"I'm sorry," Sam said.

"So am I, friend, so am I." He sighed. "But that's neither here nor there. We sold the house in Seattle and banked the money and came east. I'm originally from Brooklyn, myself, and I like the east and I wanted to get away from Seattle. Everything reminded me of the old lady."

"I see." Money in the bank! Let's go! "What kind of house were you looking for, Mr. Thompson? Just for the two of you?"

"Call me Chief. I was a Chief Petty Officer until I retired ten years ago. Got married. Married an older girl with some money. Not older than me, of course, but no chick, either. Anyway, she got the big C and died on me last fall. I can tell you it was one hell of a hit on the head, Mister . . . ?"

"Deitsch. Sam Deitsch. Call me Sam."

"You Jewish, Sam?"

"Yup," Sam said.

"Good. I like dealing with Jews. You always know where you stand and big numbers don't scare them. I'd like something on the water, big enough for me and the boy and a cook and maybe a cleaning woman. Not too far from the railroad, either. I'll be going to New York a lot and I don't like driving any more. Can't see at night, to tell the truth."

"Well, I'll be honest with you, Chief," Sam said. "A house on the water up this way costs an arm and a leg."

"How much is an arm and a leg?"

"Quarter of a million, three hundred thousand." Sam spread his hands to show how hopeless it all was.

"Well, that's an arm and a leg, all right, but I think we can manage it. Do you have some pictures or something we can look at here? I mean I don't want to drive all over hell's half acre looking at places that don't make any sense in the first place."

Sam bent down and opened the lower right hand drawer of his desk. He took out a box of colored slides depicting the many white elephants that had come to High Ridge Realty. He got up. "If you and your son will come into the meeting room, we'll take a look at some of these." Sam led the way, thinking, *Good old generous Doug sloughed another deadbeat on me and I'm going to sell him a million dollars worth of house.* He forced himself to put off figuring his commission until later, so his mind would not be cluttered or panicked now. The boy and the big man sat on opposite sides of the long table, looking at the screen while Sam showed pictures of some of the most expensive housing in America.

One was the Sargent house, a big classy old rambling ruin with an acre of lawn behind it and beyond the lawn Long Island Sound. "What's that one?" the Chief asked.

"That's the Sargent house," Sam said. He read from the notes. "Two-acre waterfront. Six bedrooms, four baths. Boathouse and dock, squash courts . . ."

"What are they asking?"

"Two-sixty-five."

"Whoo, that's a lot of money." The Chief's eyes rested on the boy thoughtfully. "You like it?" The boy smiled and nodded. "It's his money much as it is mine. *More* than it's mine," the Chief said. "Let's go take a look. Maybe he can learn to play squash or whatever."

They drove out to the Sargent place in the Chief's car, a solid Mercedes. Sam let them in through the kitchen door. "Run around, take a look," the Chief said to the boy. The boy ran off. Sam and the Chief toured the house and the grounds. "Think they'll take two-fifty?" the Chief asked.

"I'm sure they'll take two-fifty," Sam said.

"All right. Let's get back to town." They rounded up the boy and Sam locked the door and they left. On the way back to the office, the Chief was quiet, even morose. Perhaps the house and the water reminded him of his lost wife. At the office, the Chief announced he was going to get deposit money, and would leave the boy as security. He laughed.

"Today's Saturday," Sam reminded him. "The banks are closed today."

The Chief winked, and smiled a wet, secret smile under his beard. "Not this bank," he said. He got in the Mercedes, winked again, and drove off.

Sam took the boy back to his office and heaped magazines on his lap. The boy let his large head fall forward as he studied *Life*. Sam reckoned his commission on the client Doug Hamilton had thrown away to be $6,850, even with expenses and splits. He had made it, turned the corner. He was in the clear. An hour passed, and then two hours, and it was seven and twilight and the poor kid was bored stiff. Sam tried to entertain him. "Does your father go away and leave you like this often?" he said with a light laugh.

"He's not my father." It was the first time Sam had heard the boy speak, and his voice was cracked and shrill.

"He's not your father?" Sam smiled. "Who is he?"

"I don't know."

"You," Sam said, pointing hard at the boy. "You. You don't know who he is? The Chief?"

"No. He picked me up after school. We've been driving for days and days."

"Oh. Oh boy. What school? Where are you from?"

"Eastman Junior High."

"Where's that?" Sam said.

"Seattle."

"Seattle? And you don't know who he is?"

"Yes, sir, Seattle, and no, sir, I don't know who he is."

"Ah," Sam said. "Ah." He lifted the phone slowly, and slowly dialed the police. God hurry summer, when he could make dresses and money again.

The letter was four typewritten pages from Bobby, the son who played football at Delaware. Carmody spread the pages across the kitchen table, then picked up the sheet that contained the message and guts of the letter.

". . . too establishment-jock, so I have decided to quit the team. I'm not doing this without thinking. I like football and spring training was a gas. The guy in front of me is a senior but he tackles like a turnstile, so I'll be first string next fall, after they see the first game films. Or I would be, but I'm quitting. When you think of the energy expended playing football, and the lumps you take, and for what? For nothing but a stupid game, really, when the whole world is falling down around your ears. Why not take some of the energy and go out and work with the street kids? And if you have to take lumps, why not get them in Chicago, from the police?

"My decision is made, actually. I'm writing you about it now so when you hear I've quit from the coaches or somebody, you'll know why I quit and not think I was chicken or sore because I couldn't make the first team or something. I'm also writing you because if I don't play football, it will probably cost you some money next year and the year after. Or I'll have to ask for some, I should say. I don't think they'll take my scholarship away, because it wasn't all football, anyway. But they're not going to support me in the style I was just becoming accustomed to if I don't play ball. No more alumni sending checks or letting you run a bill at their tailor's or gas station, so I will probably need some money. I read the papers and I know things are tough everywhere, that there's a recession and all, and I know they're especially tight with you, what with cigarette commercials dead, but I hope you'll be able to put up some money so I can do what I think I ought to do. I want to do it, and you always said a good man was a man who wanted to do what he thought he ought to do. I don't think I'll have to bother you until fall. I'll be working with street kids in Wilmington and they're paying me something. But if you send a check, I won't send it back without cashing it, I . . ."

"You're all right, kid," Carmody said to the empty kitchen. "Writes a nice letter, too." He assembled the letter in a small pile before him. "Money," he said. "Fucking *money!*" He slammed his fist down on the letter. "Just balls and bullshit!" He sighed and sat back in his chair, a monologue beginning. "As for your fine fantasy about an apartment in the City, Carmody, forget it. You set too much in motion too long ago, and you have responsibilities you cannot walk away from. The next letter might be from young Jack in Munich asking for money and you should by

God have money to send him. And Helen, for all she's a pain in the ass and it's great to have her out of the house, shouldn't be scrounging in some crummy office for a hundred a week.

"No, Jack-me-bye, it's time to type a resumé and put it through mimeo and start hustling around employment agencies and get yourself a decent job. Hold your hat in your hand and bend your creaking knee. It will do your soul good.

"Ooooo! Oho! Oh, Jesus, I hate to do it! There're dozens of them out there will set up interviews just for the chance to let Jack Carmody have it in the teeth. Well. That's life, lad. Live it. Unless somebody drops ten-twelve thousand dollars in your lap and there's nobody can do that. Even if your father died, he could leave only his underwear, and his buddies on the Embarcadero might steal that. Take off your hat, Carmody. Bend your knee. Get a job."

Lew Morris was in a light sweat of fear. In his early days as an actor, Harry Price had a reputation for violence, and in twenty years Lew had not seen him quite so dangerously angry as he was now. "You've just gotta believe me, Harry. I don't have it. I mortgaged off my house two years ago. I'm plain old-fashioned broke."

"You've *got* to get it," Harry said harshly. Even his teeth looked dangerous. "My wife put up ten grand and she's a Hollywood *act*ress! I've got to put up matching money or I can't go home! If I go home without it, she'll bug me crazy!"

For the tenth or twelfth time, Lew Morris said, "There's a terrific depression out here, Harry. Not a recession. Nothing nice like in the newspapers. This town's broker than in nineteen-thirty, thirty-one. Marlon Brando's looking for work. Kirk Douglas. . ."

"Brando! Douglas! They don't know what broke is!" Harry quieted suddenly. "Lew, look. I want you to regard this as the most important money you ever tried to raise in your life. Like it was your kid's ransom, or an operation to save your sight. I have got to have ten grand to match what Betsy put up. Or I will kill her."

"I have six hundred dollars in the world," Morris said. He took a big checkbook from his desk. "It's all I have, believe me, in the world right now, and it's yours. More than that, Harry, I cannot do."

"I'll see you around, Lew," Harry said, and he got up like jumping and raced out of the office.

In the corridor, striding toward the elevator, Harry cooled, and he remembered a curious and sad thing he had said to Lew Morris. *I have got to match what Betsy put up or I will kill her.* It didn't make much sense, but it was perfectly true.

He was suddenly plunged over an edge of sadness at the thought of killing Betsy, because if he killed her they would put splendid Harry Price, television pioneer, in a cell and throw away the key.

Nothing in the curricula at St. George's or Dartmouth had prepared Sandy Campbell for what he was about to do, which was recruit bank robbers. Did you meet in a dungeon, lit by a candle in a wine bottle, and plot? Did you approach each man clandestinely, talking out of the side of your mouth about a "job"? Not if you were a former vice president of The Bank Street Fund, you didn't. However, Sandy had learned a lot since Dartmouth, and learned most of it at The Bank Street Fund, and at the Fund, when they wanted to contact mature men to make a business proposition, they set up a lunch. Absolutely without irony, simply because it was the only process he knew and understood, Sandy arranged for a private luncheon in The Haig Room of the Southport Country Club, and he invited three acquaintances, Jack Carmody, Sam Deitsch, and Harry Price. With nothing else in the world to do (Sam did not go to High Ridge Realty since reporting a kidnapping), and impelled by great curiosity, all three accepted at once.

There were drinks and golf- and kid-talk, and small steaks with salads, and over coffee, when the waiters had cleared the table and left the room, Sandy began, inevitably, "I suppose you're all wondering why I called you together today."

6

On Selecting
a Wheelman for a Heist

"I'LL LAY IT ON THE LINE for you, put all my cards on the table, and try to be as honest as I know how," Sandy began. "Nobody has to tell any of you that times are tough, that what the President calls a recession is a depression, and there's no money around and very few jobs. The unusual thing about this depression, it seems to me, is that it affects men like us—competent men accustomed to good positions and high salaries. We have been hard hit, and there's no light at the end of the tunnel right now that I can see.

"To be, as I say, as honest as I know how, let me begin by saying I felt a terrific cash pinch about a month ago and went down to collect unemployment insurance. I applied in New Canaan because my house is right on the Westport line, and I didn't want to be seen standing in line in Westport. I'm sure you'll all understand that. I might add I don't feel especially proud of going on unemployment, and I keep explaining to my-self that it's money I have coming after all the taxes I paid when I

was making a decent salary. But how I feel about accepting unemployment compensation is neither here nor there, has nothing
to do, except marginally, with what I have to say here. I want only
to establish that I went on unemployment, and I should add I
welcome that check every Saturday.

"The point of my going on unemployment, as it affects us here,
is that I didn't want to go down and cash the check with Tom
Burrell at the Westport Trust because he might not understand
and might tell somebody—what the hell, he'd certainly tell his
wife—and the news might get back to my wife, who's insecure
enough right now, and she'd be worried sick. So I drove around
with my first check in my pocket, and I found a bank across the
state line from New Canaan, in New York, in a small bend in the
road called Vista. Maybe you've seen it." There were muttered
No's, and the shaking of heads.

"All right. The bank at Vista is part of a great big supermarket
shopping plaza that nobody goes to. Trust me on this, nobody.
The parking lot is deserted in the middle of the day. Just *no*-
body goes there. The place was so empty I honestly thought at
first there had been an air raid or something, but no. Just nobody
ever goes to the Vista shopping plaza, or whatever they call it. I
thought it was an ideal place to cash my unemployment check
without anybody, especially my wife, finding out. I went in and
made arrangements with the manager, a fellow named Hayden.
He's been cashing my unemployment checks regularly since. . . .
Does anybody have a cigarette?" There was a stir, and Carmody
pushed a pack of Old Gold Filter Kings across the table, with
matches on top.

Sandy lit up. "First in more than a year," he said. "Anyway.
Every monday morning for three-four weeks I've been driving
through this empty parking lot to stop my car, all alone and by
itself, in front of this bank, and I go in and there's nobody there.
No customers, that is. Just three tellers and an old guard and the
manager. . . ."

Carmody thought, *Shit, I should go up there with a gun and knock the joint over.*

"Three tellers, girls, an old guard, and the manager," Sandy said again. At The Bank Street Fund one learned that repetition was an effective form of emphasis. "Yet they have as much money around as any bank, I suppose. God knows how much that would be, but I assume it's a lot. There are no customers, the guard is an old, skinny man, the manager is a lightweight. . . ." His head was spinning from the cigarette and he put it out brusquely.

"What I propose, gentlemen, is that the four of us join forces and rob the Vista bank."

If a good stunning can produce a kind of silence, then the silence that fell might be described as stunned. Carmody and Deitsch looked at one another in untempered wonder. Rob, a, bank. The wonder was compounded because the proposal came from a man with no reputation for practical jokes, came from a man without a track record for special humor. Came from Sanford Campbell, Brady Iselin's devoted husband, father of Rachel and young Sandy and Rocky Campbell, a former vice president of The Bank Street Fund, PTA stalwart noted for tennis and sailing, Republican, WASP.

"Well, thanks a whole lot for the lunch," Sam said, "but I have a new career in real estate which—"

"You have no place to go but the police station," Sandy said, "to discuss a curious abduction. If you liked the lunch, give me half an hour."

"If I may, I'd like to ask a question," Carmody said drily. "Have you considered that being out of work has addled you? Made you a little screwy?" He added, to take the sting out, "It's a trial, I know. I've been going a little screwy myself."

"That's true," Sandy said. "I've done my homework on this thing, and I know you're a little screwy right now. But I'm not."

"I have a question, too," Harry Price said. "Why didn't you tell me you had something like this in mind when you called me? I'm busy. I have work to do afternoons."

"No, you don't," Sandy said. "You don't have a thing to do. You received no money for your last picture and there's no money for new pictures."

"How did you know that?" Price said.

"I told you I've done my homework."

Sam introduced better manners. "Well, ah, Sandy, you seem to have it all pretty well thought out. Perhaps you could tell us what you have in mind."

"Nothing elaborate," Sandy said. "Just a run-of-the-mill bank job. Guns, ski masks, three men to hit the bank and one man outside with the motor running. Split the money four ways. Go home and forget about it."

"Just like that," Carmody said calmly.

"Yes, as a matter of fact, *just* like that. I've thought about it from every angle, with every contingency. We cannot miss. Hit the bank some Monday morning and beat it." Sandy took another Old Gold from Carmody's pack and lit it. "I trust simplicity," he said. "If you people see anything complex in the plan, tell me and we'll drop it."

"Well, it's just silly, that's all, Sandy," Harry Price said. "Christ, here we are, four grown family men in an expensive club talking about robbing a bank." He shook his head hard. "It's just silly, that's all."

"It's worse than silly, it's absurd," Sandy said. "That's why nobody will be looking for us. Most police arrests, I understand, are made on information from stool pigeons. I doubt very much that the police have informers operating inside the Southport Country Club."

"But I've never even knocked over a candy store," Carmody said. "I don't even shoplift. I don't know how I'd behave."

Sandy put out his second cigarette before he got hooked again. "That's too bad. I was depending on you. Two hundred days in the line, field commission, mentioned in dispatches, decorated. Lieutenant Colonel in the National Guard . . ."

"Well, you *have* done your homework," Carmody said.

"Then, of course," Sam said, voice of doom, "there's prison and disgrace and loss of everything for all of us." He was purely dismayed, thinking of separation from his daughter Lisa.

"I've thought of that, too," Sandy said, "and what I decided is undemocratic and un-American and nobody will like it less than I do, but it's a fact. Suppose for a minute we do get caught. And suppose also, which is imperative, that nobody gets shot in this thing. Then it's four men of substance and accomplishments driven temporarily mad by the Nixon recession, who have taken money from a small bank. We return the money, plead guilty to save the state expense, and at the worst do a couple of years. Probably get suspended sentences. As to the disgrace, I've learned it's a bigger disgrace to be broke in this town than to be crooked."

"I understand the courts are so backed up that they don't get to you for a couple of years," Sam said hopefully. "Until then you're out on bail."

"You saw it on television. About four years ago, right?" Harry Price said to Sam.

"Well, now you bring it up, yes," Sam said.

"It was an NBC white paper. I produced that show," Harry said. "The courts are backed up for nobodies. We're somebodies. We get caught in a thing like this and the papers will go out of their minds and every judge on the Connecticut bench will be dying, take my word dying, to try this case and throw the book at us. There'll be no delay. You want a delay, be nobody or black or both."

"I must admit I hadn't thought of that," Sandy said.

"I've been thinking a lot about jail lately," Price said enigmatically, remembering Betsy. "And I think armed robbery beats murder every way. I'd like to talk again."

"What about you two?" Sandy said to Deitsch and Carmody. "Not do you want to rob a bank right away, but do you want to talk again?" Deitsch and Carmody paused together, then nodded in curious unison. Even their nods were alike, left ear foremost, like music critics listening. "All right. Thank you for joining me at lunch, gentlemen. I'll call you all later in the week. Now let's go to the bar and have a small drink on it." They moved to the table before the fireplace, where there were a half-dozen bottles, but talk was meager, and not even Jack Carmody stayed very long.

Harry Price was on his third wife and hadn't talked to the first two, either. Jack Carmody never told anybody much anyway. But Sam Deitsch had lived in fullest intimacy with his wife for twenty-one years, and he was swollen with information when he got home. He looked like a tonsured cherub, eyes glistening with a holy light, when he walked into the kitchen. Joanna was baking, an old passion she indulged now frequently in the name of economy and at great expense. Her face was flushed from the oven's heat, and her hair fell in fetching tendrils along her damp cheeks. "You sold a house," she said, and ran at Sam and kissed him.

"No, no. I don't even go to the office any more." He kissed Joanna and turned away.

She would not let go. "You saw Milton?" She nodded earnestly. "You saw Milton and he gave you a check?"

"How could I see Milton? Drive to Orange, New Jersey, and back in three hours? Impossible." Sam pried himself loose.

"Did you get a job or something?"

"No. Nothing. It's nothing."

Joanna turned back to the stove. "Don't bang your feet like a mad elephant. I got a cake in."

"I'm standing still!" Sam said. They fought, as has been noted, without skill, but even the most vicious marital infighter would not have used Sam's next line. "It's something, yes. I have something. But I can't tell you about it now, and probably never."

Joanna was so entirely caught by her feminine roots that she looked at Sam sharply, to see if it was a deliberate joke, a put-on. It wasn't, and curiosity plunged to her bowels and roiled there. "As long as you bring some money home," she said, and rechecked her dials and creations. Sam could not make himself leave the kitchen. "Will it bring some money home?" Joanna asked, when she could be silent no longer.

"A lot of money. But I can't tell you about it," Sam said. After more than twenty years of intimacy, secretiveness comes clumsily, if at all.

"All right. Don't tell me. It's probably some crazy scheme you're ashamed of anyway."

"You won't be ashamed to spend the money!"

"Don't shout! I got a cake in! Get out of my kitchen and plot the overthrow of the government while I cook!"

Sam went to the cellar door and down the stairs. He would be sleeping alone for a while now, but it was just as well. Joanna knew so much about him that he sometimes suspected he talked in his sleep.

The Iselin family had had so much money for so long that the men took up teaching and poetry. There were philosopher Iselins and sculptor Iselins, and several men of a more worldly view had become career diplomat Iselins. They were none of them frugal, and they gave well and wisely to each other, and to universities and charities. The inevitable occasional wastrel was staked to a start in Chile or Australia, where the Iselins are big today. When the poet or the diplomat needed money, he wrote to Aunt Sarah, or whoever was reigning at the time, and said how much he needed and why, and a transaction was made.

So Brady Iselin Campbell worried about money the way whites worry about white-only facilities. She knew there could be trouble in that area somewhere, but she didn't fret about it, really, at all. And nothing in her husband's constitution wished to challenge or alter that serenity. They sat at cocktails in a large, clean living room. "Christ, I hate drinking in the middle of the day," Sandy said. "It makes me fuzzy and cross as hell."

"Did you take some aspirin? That generally helps," Brady said.

"Makes one eye hazy," Sandy said. "What generally works best is more booze." He went to a table and put more whisky in his glass. "You, ah, wouldn't have anything left out of that check I gave you Saturday, would you?"

"The thousand from Connie? Well, some. I had to pay Julio something, our bill there is enormous, and I paid Doctor Entzel a hundred . . ."

"Oh, I don't want an accounting, love. I just wondered if there was anything left. I have a thing going that will need some money."

"There should be about seven hundred dollars left," Brady said. "I *think*."

"Would you mind if I took about four hundred of it? Short-term loan, is all it is."

"Of course not."

"Or maybe four-fifty, if you can spare it."

"Sure. Is that what the business lunch was all about?" Brady wasn't prying, only making conversation, and you were supposed to show interest in your husband's work.

"Yes. I'll be making a big deposit in a week or two. If you can endure franks and beans a little longer, I think we'll be all right soon."

"I *love* franks and beans, but we're having venison tonight. Elaine Carleton's freezer broke down."

Sandy threw back his head and laughed, clearing all the crossness and the fuzz. It was so absurd to be rich and not have any money. "I love venison," he said.

"I know you do," Brady said, just a little impatiently. "I didn't know you found it amusing, too."

They met at noon Sunday in a guest cottage a hundred feet to the rear of the Campbell home. Three of the aspirant thieves had never seen the cottage before, and they were not surprised to find an electric IBM typewriter and a Xerox copier on a vast rectangular table, nor did they remark that the telephones had labeled buttons. "Nice place," Sam Deitsch said. "Off in the woods. Wouldn't even know it was here unless somebody showed you."

"My name is on that box," Carmody said. "Sorry, I can't see my name without reading it."

Sandy gave the box to Carmody, and gave boxes to Deitsch and Price. "These are business cards. I had them engraved. I made you vice president, Jack, and Harry secretary and Sam treasurer."

"What am I vice president of now?" Carmody asked, opening his box.

"An outfit called Four Talents, Limited. We are incorporated in Delaware for tax purposes. This is our letterhead." Sandy took sheets from the top of a sheaf and passed them around. "I think it's kind of handsome."

"A cable address," Sam said. "Very stylish."

"Why secretary?" Harry Price asked. "I can't even type."

"I was going to make you president and myself secretary," Sandy said, "but I'm the only one here who's not posted, not publicly broke, you know . . ."

"Posted," Carmody said. "Is that where you got my name?"

"So I made myself president to make the outfit look solvent," Sandy continued. "Yes, Jack. I got all your names from the posted list."

"Goddam," said Carmody.

"I shouldn't be on that list," Price said. "I'm *sure* I sent those bastards a check."

"I thought you wanted me for my brain," Sam said.

Sandy took the original posted list from his pocket and tossed it on the table. "That's where I got your names. I don't know why my name's not on it, I'm far enough behind. Anyway, I was down at the bank to have some Four Talents checks printed, and Tom Burrell asked if I could use a new business loan. I figured why not, and took twelve hundred dollars from him. I rented that typewriter over there and the Xerox and a Dictaphone and had the phone company put in two lines under new numbers. I also went down and talked to Meyer, at the Club, and until further notice we can all sign bar tabs with our names and Four Talents."

"You know, you're smarter than you look," Carmody said. "You fix the Club bills so we'll all start out saying Yes—"

"That's just business," Sandy said.

"Don't tell me, I invented it. And when you start out saying Yes, it's very difficult to turn around and say No. Then you get a typewriter and a Xerox and business cards and letterhead stationery, so that what is really a criminal assault appears to be a legitimate business enterprise." Carmody stopped, out of breath.

"It's the only way I know how to do things, Jack. Would you like a drink?"

"I should say no, if only for the practice, but yes. Badly and always. Where's the stuff?"

"In the cabinet over there," Sandy said, pointing. "What I thought we'd do today is run over to Vista and look at the bank and the shopping plaza. It's Sunday, and four grown men in a car won't attract the attention they'd attract during the week. . . ."

"I'll drive," Sam said quickly. "I haven't had an accident or a moving violation in twenty years."

"Are you kidding?" Price said. "I was a racer. Sebring, Lime Rock, Bridgehampton. I'll drive the car."

Sandy waited for Carmody to volunteer to be driver, but the big man was fixing a drink, and perhaps he realized that whatever his function in this operation, it would not be to sit outside the bank with the motor running. "Just for today, I'll drive," Sandy said. "It's my car and I know the way. We'll figure out who's going to be driver later on." Sandy would of course be driver when they hit the bank because he was known at the bank and because he was president of the corporation, but he saw no need to say so at the time. He took it as an encouraging measure of commitment from Price and Deitsch that they both wanted to drive. They were both close enough in their minds to an actual robbery to want to remain outside while it was going on.

They got into the Silver Cloud station wagon, Carmody with his drink in hand, and drove down the driveway to the road. "It's nine-point-one miles from here," Sandy said. "About seventeen minutes, taking it easy." They drove to Vista in complete silence. Sandy entered the parking lot and drove across it in a wide arc to emphasize the emptiness. He stopped the car before a great four-headed light fixture between the A & P and the bank. "It's completely empty because it's Sunday," he said. "But take my word it's just about as empty during the week. That's the bank, over there. The A-frame with the glass wall."

There was another deep silence while each man pondered his need and the risk, the absurdity of the proposition and its likelihood. Sam spoke first, wondering. "Looks like you could put a rock through the window and walk right in." "*That* would draw a crowd," Carmody said. "Fill the parking lot up in no time." "You know, I don't think they should design a bank that way," Harry Price said. "It's an open invitation for somebody to rob it. It's not fair, in a way." "Lead us not into temptation," Sam said. "I'll tell you one thing," Carmody said. "You want to rob that bank, you better hurry before somebody else does. It's asking for it."

Sandy left the big light fixture and drove in a second arc past the bank, and on to the parking lot exit. Out on the road Sam Deitsch had several proposals—Mace, smoke bombs, tear gas—all designed to circumvent the use of guns. Price speculated vaguely on seducing one of the tellers to make it an inside job. Carmody was silent, having recognized from the first that you need a gun to rob a bank. In their thinking they were all back where Sandy had been when he first saw the bank as a source of cash, but he didn't interrupt. Every idea they put forward—and even Carmody's silence—indicated increasing involvement for each of them. He let them talk.

Then Deitsch and Price got into a noisy quarrel about who was going to be wheelman, and Sandy didn't interrupt that, either. At least in their minds they had worked themselves up to the front door of the bank.

In his mind, Jack Carmody had already been in the bank, and looted it, and fled. "Just how much money do they keep in a little bank like that?" he wondered aloud. Nobody had any idea.

7

Absalom

ABOUT FIVE-POINT-NINE miles into the nine-point-one-mile drive from the Vista Plaza to the Campbell driveway, a perilous silence engulfed the car. The concept of robbing a bank was leaving the realm of speculation and intruding itself as horrid reality upon two tender sensibilities. Sandy groped for an opening line, but could fine none. He was perfectly willing to sing to break the silence, but could only think of *The Prisoner's Song*. In the silence, he waited for Deitsch or Price to speak out, and quit, in which event the project might have to be scrapped. But neither spoke, perhaps because nobody wants to be the first to show his feathers, and more probably because each expected he would be wheelman. Still in silence, they drove up the driveway to the cottage and stopped. "Well, shall we . . ." Sandy began, smiling.

"Let's get inside," Carmody said harshly. "We have work to do." He got out of the car without looking back, without shutting his door, and went to the cottage. Deitsch and Price followed, grim-faced and pale with future fear. In the cottage, Carmody went directly to the big table and started writing on a manila pad. "Sit down," he said, not looking up. *Habit of command*, Sandy thought with relief. *Help yourself.* "All right. Everybody give me your hat size and glove size and shoe size. Start with you, Sam." Deitsch and then Price and last Sandy gave him their hat and shoe sizes. Nobody knew his glove size. "Okay," Carmody said, ripping the sheet free. "Sam, you get down to the City regularly. Stop in at one of those men's stores on lower Fifth and get hats with big floppy brims and four pairs of size nine gloves. Then go to a sporting goods store and get four pairs of sneakers, those sizes. Tell them it's for adult basketball." He gave the paper to Sam, who folded and pocketed it solemnly. "The only thing that worries me is a car," Carmody said.

"I have three," Sandy said.

"Oh, Christ. Between the four of us we probably have fifteen automobiles. That isn't the problem. We need somebody else's car with somebody else's registration on a short-term loan. . . ."

"I have a pistol," Harry Price said proudly.

"Don't worry about the weapons," Carmody said. "All I have to do is sign a chit at the Armory and I can take out a tank, for Chrissakes. I'll get four carbines—"

"Just three," said Sam. "I'll be driving and I won't need one."

"Stop kidding yourself," Price said. "I have a NASCAR rating. I'll drive."

"You might as well both stop kidding yourselves," Carmody said. "We're going in. Me first and you two behind me. Sandy drives."

"I rode with him this morning," Price said. "He didn't seem like such a hot driver to me. Did he to you?"

Sam made a noise with his mouth. "All over the road," he said.

"How he drives doesn't matter. The man at the bank knows Sandy. The girls there know who he is. Somebody's bound to recognize his walk or his stance or his voice. Anything. And if they identify him, we're all dead. Sandy drives. We go in."

"I'm a damned good driver," Sandy said, outraged.

"Oh, God," Harry Price groaned. "Me go in? I don't know if I can carry it off."

Carmody laughed. "You'll carry it off, all right. I'll be right behind you." Price stared in sudden alarm, and Carmody gentled him. "Old infantry joke. Pay no heed. Tell you what I want you to do now, Harry." He pushed the manila pad and a ballpoint pen at Price. "Four Talents is going to be a television commercial production company. I think that's a sensible front nowadays. Write down in less than three pages just what that entails. Be specific and rudimentary. It's for Sam and Sandy, and they don't know the first thing." Price, his jaw still slack and his eyes not yet normal, took the pad and started writing very slowly. "This will give you two something to say about our new business venture," Carmody said to Sandy and Sam. "Probably should have started something like this with Harry long ago. Now. Sam. Can you get into New York tomorrow and buy all that stuff?"

"I guess so."

"Let's stop that right now. Yes or no."

"All right. Yes."

"Good. Bring it all here to the cottage at nine o'clock Tuesday morning. We'll get to work."

"Work?" Sandy said. "What kind of work?"

"Practice, rehearse," Carmody said. "We're dealing with green troops here, and we'll do what you always do with green troops. Drill them till they're not green any more. I'll bring weapons here Tuesday morning. We'll plan to go in the following Monday."

"What's the hurry?" Sam asked pleasantly. He was entirely prepared to postpone action—to another spring, for example.

"Somebody's going to hit that bank, and soon," Carmody said. "If it's going to be us, we'll have to hurry. That bank is asking for it. Besides. If you put off any action longer than it takes to plan and equip it, it gets bigger than the Battle of the Bulge, and twice as scary. We'll go in next Monday morning.

"But a car, dammit!" Carmody slapped at his forehead. "What the hell are we going to do for a car? We'll have to steal one, I suppose, but that's a hell of a lot tougher than it sounds. . . ."

"Maybe I can help," Sam said. He studied his hands on the table in evident misery.

"Steal a car?" Sandy cried. "You, Sam? Where would *you* steal a car?"

"I don't want to talk about it." Sam watched his hands still. "I'll let you know Tuesday morning."

Carmody shook his head. "We can't do that, Sam. If you get us a car, we have to know where it came from."

"If I have a car Tuesday, Tuesday I'll tell you about it."

"Can't you even . . . ?" Carmody began.

"No," Sam said definitely, but not loud. He was so angry he looked like a pile of rocks. "I said Tuesday." He nodded. "Tuesday."

"All right, all right," Carmody said. "Get the troops out of the hot sun. Smoke if you got 'em." He made the peace sign with both hands. "Take it easy. Tuesday's time enough. Now we need ski masks and I want a floor plan. Can you draw me a floor plan, Sandy?"

"I'm not sure. I'll draw one tomorrow, after I cash my check."

"Good. Okay," Carmody said. "And ski masks. Should we buy new ones or use what we've got?"

"Who's got a ski mask?" Harry Price said, looking up from his writing.

"I must have a half-dozen," Carmody said. "I'll bring them in. It'll draw attention, buying ski masks in June." He picked up his glass and went to the liquor cabinet by way of the refrigerator. "I think that's enough for today. Last us till Tuesday morning, anyway."

Sandy and Sam together read Harry Price's three-page prospectus for Four Talents, Ltd., the television commercial firm, and everybody had a drink. Harry and Jack Carmody got to talking about television commercial production and, yearningly, of the enormous sums men less talented than they were making on television commercials, and when the meeting broke up they decided to adjourn to the Southport Country Club to discuss matters further, and to try out their new signing privileges.

At thirteen, Rachel Campbell was a tall, bony girl with buds for breasts and an arm like a steel spring. She could throw a football thirty yards on a frozen line and throw a baseball out of sight. Sandy worried about her maturing so late in an environment that prized sexual maturity, and he worried hard, for he adored Rachel. (He would not have worried so much, nor adored her so completely, if she had been prettier, and not looked so much like her father.) But Rachel's mother, Brady, said she had been the same slow way growing up, and it hadn't mattered. Perhaps Brady was right, because the first and so far the only great tragedy in Rachel's life was when she was not permitted to play Pop Warner League football because she was a girl. She had wept bitterly over that, and the coach had taken it pretty hard too. Rachel sat now folded on the floor like a beach chair in winter, watching television. Sandy groped for a light line to open conversation, but could think of nothing. He had *The New York Times* on his lap and the six o'clock news on the set, and couldn't concentrate on either. An awful sense of portent, of dread, hung about his head and shoulders like a great wet cloak. Some forgotten but deserved calamity was about to strike all of them, and it was his fault. It was a sensation or condition he often experienced late on Sundays, and one he had long ago analyzed and dismissed. Tomorrow was a school day, and before St. George's, Sandy had been genuinely afraid of school, and there is a great deal of guilt in fear, and he had had the Sunday night blues all his life.

Rocky (Paul, and called Paul only in school) came quickly into the den, went directly to the set, and changed the channel, and started out again. Rachel hit him on the bottom with a backhand fist as he skipped for the door, laughing. "God*damm*it! *Stop* it!" Sandy roared. He could feel the blood in his cheekbones. Rocky stopped in the doorway in wonder, then fled. Rachel watched Sandy calmly, then turned back to the television. "Boy," she said. "Don't 'boy' me!" Sandy said, and bent to the *Times*, ashamed. The kids were teasing, for heaven's sake. It's their game. They do it all the time. Very gruffly, Sandy said, "Sorry," and he picked up his scotch and water and went to the living room to make himself some serious kind of goddamned bomb of a drink to drown Sunday.

His firstborn, Sanford, Jr., was sitting in the living room with a chess problem laid out before him. "Hi," he said. "Hi. How's it going?" "Fine." A long pause. "You?" "Down. Got the Sunday blues again. Decided to drown them. You want a drink?"

"No thanks," the boy said, altogether uninterested.

Sandy made himself a suicidal martini-rocks. "Funny how things change. When I was your age and my father offered me a drink, I dived for it."

Young Sandy looked something up in *The Master's Manual*. "Know what they call drinkers now?" he said. "The kids, I mean?"

"No. What do they call drinkers?"

"Juice freaks." He moved a chess piece.

"Juice freaks?"

"Yes. Like speed freaks or pot heads. Juice freaks." He laughed.

"Oh. Well, I'll be in the den in case any of the kids show up and want a kick in the pants." He left ungraciously.

"Right-O," Sandy Jr. said.

It was absolutely dishonest to tell yourself you liked all of your kids equally. Nobody likes any given group of people equally. It was also unfair to the kid you favored and the kid you didn't favor not to recognize your feelings and adjust. As long as you loved them equally, which was possible because you loved without reasons, but you needed reasons to like somebody. He went into the den and swallowed a lot of his gin and picked up the *Times* to try again. Rachel turned and smiled at him in some intimate complicity, and his heart dropped. Was that what had started all the guilt tonight? Watching Rachel, whom he adored, never mind favored? Was that the guilt that had fathered this crazy dread?

No. Of course not, stupid. It was the bank. You, Sanford Campbell, are planning to steal money from somebody. Not to give to the poor, but spend on yourself and your family. And for all you have recruited accomplices to share the action, you neglected to recruit somebody to share the guilt. You feel guilty because you are a criminal. Simple as that. Okay. Now that you've figured it out, try smiling. "There's a big piece on Joe Namath here, honey," he said to Rachel.

She unfolded from the floor like a skeleton on a string. "Where!"

"In the magazine section. Here." He handed it to her. Rachel grabbed the magazine and refolded on the floor, rapt. My love, the love of my life, is mad for Joe Namath and what, as they said at St. George's, will ye do in the end thereof?

Betsy Price had an assortment of different characters she could be at will, and after three minutes with Helen Carmody she became Eve Arden, sardonic sidekick to the Love Interest. (Betsy didn't know that Helen was also an assortment of characters, or that she had no control over which one she would be.) They were four together at cocktails on a vast veranda overlooking the Woodbury Course. Price and Carmody were talking television with the intensity and elation of mutual discovery. Betsy and Helen made do admirably. "Sid Kransky," Betsy said. "Did you hear that? He drops one more name, I'm going to lose lunch."

"I haven't been listening. Did Jack mention President Kennedy yet?"

Betsy shook her head. "Not yet. I'm sure I would have noticed. He knocked me out."

"He will. Jack was a consultant for the Kennedy campaign. On television commercials."

"Wow. That *is* a good drop. Let me know if he uses it. I want to hear what Harry says back."

"Personally, I'd be impressed if he could drop Paul Newman or John Lindsay." Helen kissed at the air.

"I know he has a Newman," Betsy said. "He's probably saving it." And they chat on like that, civilized and friendly.

After two drinks at the bar, Price and Carmody had gotten on strong Harry-and-Jack terms, and had decided to invite their wives to the Club for dinner. Both had been in and around business long enough to know that such intimacy can imperil the sturdiest enterprise, but they had had drinks, and had been high on hope and excitement, so they had invited the girls.

Now, on the veranda, with everybody getting along so well they had to speak by turns, the worry and reservation seemed silly. They ordered dinner served in the dining room, and just for the hell of it had an extra round of drinks sent to the table. They finished drinks on the veranda, and Betsy and Helen leading the way, chatting amiably, they went into the dining room. At the table they paired off in a traditional and agreeable way, Betsy talking to Jack Carmody and Helen asking Harry about movies and stars. The last drink was just barely one too many for everybody, but just barely, so they had a fine evening together. Harry and Jack both grabbed for the check, and in the end both signed it, adding "Four Talents" at the bottom. There was a moment's hesitation at the cashier's desk, during which Carmody and Price made scared little-boy faces at each other, but the tab cleared and they had a brandy in the bar before going home.

However, of the many people Helen Carmody was, tonight the mistress or lover side of her nature was ascendant, and she looked at her husband frequently in such a sexy way that Betsy looked twice and three times at Jack to see what was so exciting, and of course she found much. He was big, with powerful hands and an awesome masculinity, none of which she would have noticed if Helen hadn't been looking at him as though she were his mistress.

Harry noticed between movie star anecdotes the way Betsy was looking at Carmody, and he was miffed, and Helen, who had noticed nothing, unaccountably turned into the Crazy Lady on the drive home and told Jack he had made a fool of himself slobbering drunkenly over poor Betsy Price, which gave Carmody ideas he had not earlier entertained. When the Prices got home, Betsy put on an outrageous nightgown, obtained by mail from an exotic catalogue, in order to shatter Harry's manhood further, but thanks to the Vista bank venture and the television commercial prospects, Harry's confidence was intact and he was Highpockets McStud to her vamp. Betsy was too surprised for pleasure, and became suspicious and withdrawn.

Organizations that impose celibacy on their rank and file sometimes endure for centuries.

Monday morning. Halfway across the imitation marble floor of the Vista branch of the Westchester County Trust Company, Mister Sanford Campbell's loose, confident, manly stride broke as though a trick knee had buckled. A large, strange, serious man sat at Malcolm Hayden's desk. Behind him, at other desks and tables, were other men in dark suits. All of the strange men were solemnly busy. Sandy regained his stride in part and continued on to the receptionist's desk. "Good morning," she said, smiling anxiously.

"Good morning. Is Mister Hayden in?" Sandy looked around at the tellers, who were trying to seem occupied, and at the guard, who no longer slouched in a corner but stood at a resolute Parade Rest in the center of the floor.

"Whom shall I say is here, please?" the girl said loudly, for somebody else's benefit.

"Mister Campbell. I come here every Monday morning."

The receptionist pointed at a chair. "Won't you be seated? I'll see if Mister Hayden is free." She went to a door right rear of the bank and knocked and went in. Sandy had not noticed the door before, and watched sharply. It opened on a conference room, where more men were solemnly busy. He also saw that at the left rear of the bank was a thick steel door, open to show a complex lock mechanism and beyond the door a vault. He noted these in his mind.

Hayden followed the anxious girl out of the conference room. Sandy stood to meet him, and they shook hands. "Is it about your check?" Hayden said, almost in a whisper.

"Yes."

"Come on over here a minute, if you would." Hayden led the way to a customers' counter. He took Sandy's check and initialed it. "Bank examiners," he said, as in "Cheese it, the cops."

"But you just opened this branch, didn't you?"

"They come at random," Hayden said. "They might be back next week, although the odds are enormous. Oh," he added, remembering something. "I wanted to speak to you. . . ."

"Go ahead," Sandy said. He welcomed the extra time to look around the bank.

"No. Not today. There's just too much going on here today. Will you be in next Monday?"

"Next Monday?" Sandy stiffened straight up.

"To cash your check." Hayden smiled.

"Oh, certainly."

"Fine. Next Monday then. Thanks, Mister Campbell." Hayden hurried off waving.

"Next Monday," Sandy said after him. He went to a teller's window and cashed the check. His hand trembled as he picked up the money. Next Monday. He would have to come to this bank on Monday, after robbing it, and walk through a host of cops to cash his unemployment check at a bank whose money would be—God willing—in his guest cottage at the time.

Hayden wanted to speak to him about something, would be looking for him, might find it curious if he didn't show. If Carmody knew about it, or figured it out, he would insist that Sandy go back, after they had hit the bank. He would have to convince Carmody to put off the operation for a day, at least.

That was when he became aware, with a twinge of something not yet strong enough to recognize, that it was not his robbery any more, and Carmody was in charge.

Monday afternoon, late. Sam Deitsch opened the trunk of his Cadillac and put the basketball sneakers in with the gloves and the big floppy hats and he shut the trunk and got in the front seat of the car and sat still for a long time.

Then Sam started the Cadillac and drove south on Park Avenue through Union Square and on south to where he turned east into a section he had called "uptown" as a boy. Sam knew the section well and he drove not rapidly but confidently and without delay to an address on Fourth Street near Avenue "C" in a neighborhood distinguished by filth.

Sam got out of his car and locked it and stepped over rubbish and garbage and through a doorway with no door in it. Thick odors struck him in the face. In the dark of the hall, two splendid motor-cycles stood chained to themselves and each other and to a radiator. Sam climbed the stairs to the second floor and knocked on the door of the rear apartment. A young man with very long black hair and a stringy beard came to the door and said, "It's you. Come in," and Sam said, "You alone, Jerry?" and the young man said, "No," and Sam said, "Come outside and talk," and Jerry stepped into the hall and shut the door behind him. "What's up?" he said.

Sam said, "I need a car. Somebody else's car and I need it Wednesday. Can you help me?" and Jerry laughed and said, "You? . . . Sure. How much?" and Sam said, "A hundred now, two hundred on delivery," and the young man said, "Where?" and Sam said, "Greenwich railroad station," and Jerry said, "Three o'clock. Park and wait. You got the hundred?"

And Sam took an envelope from his pocket and gave it to the

young man. "Will you be delivering it, Jerry?" Jerry said, "I don't know. Maybe," and Sam said, "Then maybe I'll see you there," and Jerry said, "In that case, no. Somebody else will deliver. So long, Sam," and Sam said, "So long, son."

And Sam went down the evil stairs and out to the Cadillac he had hustled and sweated for and turned it north toward the suburb he had hustled and sweated for, and he might have thought "Absalom my son, my son Absalom," but he had thought that years ago and now he didn't know what to think.

8

Tuesday Morning

JACK CARMODY, in his eagerness, arrived at the Campbell cottage before nine on Tuesday to discover Sandy making Xerox copies of a handwritten will. Carmody had a thick sheaf of shopping bags under one arm, and suspended from his other hand a shopping bag with small rifle barrels poking from it. "Twenty-five cents apiece!" he said, dropping the sheaf of bags on the table. "I remember when these were called 'two-cent bags.' I remember when they were free, for Chrissakes!" He saw a sheet peel off the Zerox. "Is that the floor plan?"

"No," Sandy said. "It's nothing."

"Oh, a will. You don't need a will for this thing. A walk in the sun."

"I don't want to die intestate because it sounds like something was cut off," Sandy said. "Here's the floor plan. Needless to say, I drew it myself."

"Crude but serviceable," Carmody said. "I see. The tellers

there," he began pointing around the room, "and the manager there. That's a conference room." He pointed at the door to the bunk room. "We'll have to make sure that's empty. Grab the other end of the table, old man, and we'll put it along the wall to simulate the tellers' counter."

They moved furniture around the large central room—the living room-kitchen—of the cottage to represent bank fixtures. Sandy took orders joylessly, acceding to Carmody's wishes. The habit of command was beginning to stir not a resentment, but a certain undeniable restlessness. "Now that's the vault," Carmody said, pointing at the bathroom door. "You say it was open yesterday. What was inside?"

"A laundromat." Sandy was sorry he said it.

"No kidding! A laundromat?"

"Of course not, Jack. How the hell do I know what was inside? I couldn't just stroll over to their vault and take a look around."

"I see," Carmody said. The troops were tense. "I thought perhaps you could see in from there." He pointed at the chair that represented Hayden's desk. "Never mind. Here come the Westport Strolling Players. We can get to work."

Harry Price and Sam Deitsch arrived together in Deitsch's car. There were subdued greetings all around, and coffee was poured. Carmody explained the disposition of the furniture and the bank layout. Then he gave everybody a carbine and began, "Gentlemen, this is your rifle. It is your only friend. It is your wife. You will eat with it, and sleep—"

"Come off it," Sam said. "I must have heard that lecture a dozen times. This isn't basic training."

"That's the way the assembly-disassembly talk begins," Carmody said. "It's in all the manuals."

"Assembly-disassembly," Harry Price said. "I don't care if it comes apart or not as long as nobody puts any bullets in it."

"A gun is to shoot!" Carmody said, outraged. "You never point a gun at a man unless you mean to kill him! Point an empty gun at a man, he doesn't know it's empty, he's got a right to kill you! No bullets?" Carmody became so moved he lost speech.

"Let him kill me. It's better than jail," Price said. He had directed a Group W special on the penal system and was deathly afraid of homosexual rape. "But no bullets in *my* gun."

"Well, we got all day and we got all week," Sandy said, "so let's kill a little time at the start by taking the carbine apart and putting it back together again. Personally, I like guns."

"I do, too," Sam said.

Carmody took a deep breath. "All right. We will dispense with the nomenclature, gentlemen. Seizing the barrel of the weapon in the left hand and employing a screwdriver or knife or a dime, the ten-cent piece . . ." Carmody showed them how to take the carbine apart and put it together again. His most enthusiastic pupil was Harry Price, who had never been any kind of recruit, and had always thought guns were all one piece.

When the guns were reassembled and put aside, Carmody again explained the layout of the room and of the bank. "Did you get the hats and sneakers and all that stuff, Sam?" he asked.

"It's all outside in the trunk of my car."

"Would you get it and bring it in, please?" Carmody was calming his restless troops with good manners. He reached deep in the bag that had had carbines in it. "I brought the ski masks."

"Wait a minute," Sandy said, oddly close to laughter. "Wait just a minute. We can't run around out here with ski masks and floppy hats and sneakers. With guns in our hands. The kids will see us. Or somebody will see us and we'll all be committed before we get anywhere near jail."

"I got us a car, too," Sam said. "For tomorrow."

Carmody looked at Sandy as though he were the leader of a palace coup, then looked at Sam with alarm and dismay. He appeared briefly but definitely lunatic. "Jesus! The car!" He struck his forehead with great force. "I must be getting old. I forgot all about the car!"

"Wednesday afternoon. Three o'clock. Greenwich railroad station," Sam said.

"Oh, terrific work, Sam!" Carmody said. "Can you tell us about it?"

"You drive down with me tomorrow and pick the car up," Sam said. "I'll tell you all about it then."

"Okay, fine," Carmody said. He had figured out since Sunday that Sam would get a car through his son, Jerry. Sandy had figured it out too. Everybody knew about Sam's son Jerry, everybody in Westport except Harry Price, who commuted to Los Angeles. "Now, Sandy," Carmody said, cross. "What's this about the masks?"

"I said you're not going to run around in my back yard in masks and sneakers with guns in your hands. You're just not, that's all. Get used to it."

"Anybody sees us they'll call Hallowell," Sam said, referring to an expensive local drunk farm.

Carmody had a vision, admittedly childish but clear and cherished, of whipping three green clods in exotic costume into a disciplined fighting team. The vision was curling at the edges now like an old photograph on a smoldering log. "Well, maybe a little bit right inside here. Get the stuff anyway if you will, Sam. We'll try them on."

Sam got the equipment from the trunk of his car and brought it into the cottage. He dumped it on the floor, and everybody picked out his various sizes, and sitting on chairs and a low table, they put on basketball sneakers and gloves and ski masks. Carmody put on one of the big-brimmed hats over his ski mask and everybody laughed, and he went into the bathroom-vault to look in the mirror, and he laughed too. Then they all put on hats and postured around with carbines in their hands, laughing like small boys at recess in the anonymity of the masks, and saying, "Stick 'em up," and "All right, baby, get over against that wall."

"Don't point the guns at each other! Even if they're not loaded!"

Carmody ordered. "Now let's try this thing rough." He went to the front door and put his back against it, carbine in hand. "I'll be entering first. Sam, you and Harry get beside me here. Good. Now we'll call each other one, two, and three. No names. I'll be one, Harry you be two, and Sam you be three. We won't use any names during rehearsal and of course we won't use any names . . ."

"Why don't you be six and I'll be seven and Sam can be eight?" Harry Price said. "Then they'll be looking for a big gang."

Carmody was about to say, "Don't be silly," but he remembered these were class troops, like ROTC, and he said, "Okay. Six, seven, and eight. Now we enter together, and I go to the guard at once. Sandy, you be the guard, will you? Over there is okay. I go to the guard . . . What are you doing?"

Sam was pulling the ski mask over his head. "It itches," he explained.

"Leave it on for a couple of minutes, Sam," Carmody said winningly, belying a great impatience. "You've gotta get used to it sometime. Mine itches too." Sam pulled the mask down over his face. "Now you're the guard, Sandy, and I walk in with my head averted and my carbine in a shopping bag. Yes. That will do it. And I walk over to you like this and I say 'This is a stick-up. Give me your gun,' and I take the gun and I yell Six! Seven! Let's go! And Harry and Sam come up on either side—"

"Seven and eight. You're six," Price said.

"What?" Carmody did not at first understand. "Oh. Yes." Impatience bubbled. "Seven and eight, I yell. And eight, Sam, goes down that side, covering the tellers, to the conference room, to make sure it's empty."

"What if somebody's in there?" Sam said.

"Order them out."

"What if they won't come?"

"They'll come! They'll come!" Carmody cried. He breathed deeply. "Trust me, Sam. Now seven goes to the manager—Sandy, you be the manager now—and we herd him and everybody, including any customers, behind the counter. That table over there. Then seven and eight fill their shopping bags with money from the counter while I cover everybody. If the vault over there, the bathroom, is open, seven and eight go in there and grab what they can find. Then seven and eight go out the door and to the car and I come out last, backing to the door, covering everybody." Carmody backed up to the cottage door, carbine on his hip. He looked big and competent and menacing. A small bank could very easily be robbed with a man like that on your side.

"Okay, let's run through it again," Carmody said. "This time take the manager to the vault with you. Keep looking for contingencies, oversights. You want to take those masks off?"

"I'd just as soon get used to mine," Sam said. "I feel like somebody else with it on. Somebody braver."

"So do I," said Price. "Let's leave them on."

"All right," Carmody said. "I come in first with you two right behind me. I go to the guard. Sandy . . . ?"

They rehearsed until one, when Sandy, bored silly with being the bank guard or the somebody in the conference room and then Hayden, the manager, called a break for lunch. He suggested they have a drink there, in the cottage, if they felt like a drink, while he went downtown and got sandwiches and coffee. He was voted down most resoundingly. The opinion was all but stated that he was a very chintzy financier, taking no risks whatever and offering crumbs to his brave troops for rations. They voted three-to-one to go to Carpano's, a fine, expensive Italian restaurant on the Post Road. In order to recover esteem, Sandy paid for expenses incurred to date, and gave out generous advances, including an extra two hundred to Sam to pay for the car. Esteemed or otherwise, he had everybody sign vouchers for the cash, as in any sound business.

At a large table in the cool dark of Carpano's, the Four Talents were indistinguishable from the other prosperous middle-aged men talking business around them. They had no criminal mannerisms, and not the most experienced cop could have singled them out. In fact they talked business, like the comfortable men around them. Not the forthcoming assault on the Vista bank. That was assumed, accompli, foregone, perhaps because it was so easy in rehearsal. They went beyond Monday and talked of deals and enterprises to come. Harry Price described the several devices a film distributor can use to cheat on the gross, and how these devices could be exposed by a survey of box office receipts in the major markets. "With another ten grand for a survey I can take Kransky to court for half a million and win," he said. "Of course, collecting will be tough, and we'll probably have to settle for two-three hundred thousand. But that's a good return on the investment."

Sam Deitsch told how ten thousand (everybody seemed to have settled on that figure) could be parlayed into a quarter of a million in merchandise through Seventh Avenue financing, accounting procedures so intricate as to make Texas oil wheelers seem frugal and straightforward by comparison. "And pants suits this fall. Pants suits. I'm not cutting another skirt, long or short, for five years."

Carmody had a private use for ten thousand dollars, to implement a treasured fantasy, and he said very little except once, far from the conversation and interrupting rudely. "Jackets. We need jackets. Those blue windbreakers. 'Shells,' they call 'em. Four of them."

"I'm going to Stamford this afternoon," Sandy said. "I'll get them."

"You know the kind of windbreaker shells I mean?"

"I know exactly," Sandy said. He smiled at Carmody's intensity. "I'll get a large, two X-large and one XX-large."

"Okay," Carmody said, and fell silent again.

Except for a lot of questions, Sandy didn't contribute much to the conversation. It was just beginning to occur to him that the Four Talents front might well fund Price's survey or Deitsch's new line of pants suits. What the hell, they had all the paraphernalia.

They had driven to Carpano's in three cars, Sam transporting

Harry Price. In the midday heat of the parking lot, in the after-lunch glare, they agreed to meet again at the cottage Thursday morning at nine. Carmody said it was because he didn't want everybody to "get trained down too fine," and Sandy agreed because he didn't want to buy a forty-dollar lunch every day of the week. Sam arranged to pick Carmody up the following afternoon in time to drive to Greenwich and get somebody else's car. They parted. Sandy went to Stamford to pay parking tickets and buy four blue windbreaker shells, Carmody went to the Club to squeeze in nine holes and perhaps a quart before the day waned, and Sam drove Harry Price home.

Betsy Cameron (Etc.) Price floated in an inflatable orange arm-chair near poolside, her feet under water. She read a script bound in scarlet. Her utterly flawless smallness was wrapped scantly in a girlishly pink swimsuit. At her elbow, on the lip of the pool, a cassette played Montoya, and before the speaker was a tall slender glass of violet fluid with mint and fruit on top and a great single straw protruding. On being introduced to Sam Deitsch, she pushed large sunglasses up into her soft off-white curls and put the script ashore. "Nice to meet you, Sam," she said smiling. "Please sit down."

"Thank you," Sam said. He looked away from Betsy not so much to find a chair as simply to look away. Her perfect beauty was more than he could physically endure. "Nice to meet you, too, Betsy," he said, and seated himself.

"Would you like a drink, Sam?" Harry asked.

"No thanks," Sam said automatically. "Lunch was enough." But he was shaken then by a bitter fit of nerves in Betsy's astonishing presence.

"Some soda, then?" Betsy said. She lifted her violet drink and sipped.

"*Sure*, that's soda," Harry said. "Just don't touch a match to it."

"I didn't say this was soda," Betsy said. "And stop it, you're making Sam nervous." Betsy knew who and what was making Sam nervous. He was an odd type she recognized, as shark recognizes mark, who developed a seemingly terminal crush on her at first sight.

"All right. I'll have a scotch," Sam said. With luck, Harry poured doubles.

Harry went away and left Sam with his shattered poise and Betsy. "What do you do, Sam?" Betsy asked.

"I'm a garment manufacturer." How could he be so shaken? At his age? "Dresses."

"I thought all dress manufacturers were fat bald Jews with cigars." Betsy was teasing.

"Thanks," Sam said, "but I don't smoke." He laughed, and the laughter eased him.

Betsy laughed too. "What is a dress manufacturer doing in a business with Harry?"

"It all ties in," Sam said vaguely.

"I suppose," Betsy said. She pulled her inflatable armchair tight to the pool's side. "Here. Give me a hand," she said, reaching up.

Sam came to the side of the pool and pulled Betsy up on the tiles with a strength that surprised both of them. "Whooo!" Betsy cried, falling up against him.

"You're very light for . . ." Sam wanted to say "a build like that" but did not. "You can't weigh a hundred pounds," he said instead.

"I try to make all of it count," Betsy said, and they both laughed again. She put a terrycloth jacket over her shoulders and hugged herself in a sudden chill, popping her cleavage at Sam. "What's your part in Harry's new venture?" she asked mildly. Betty wanted desperately to know what was going on that made Harry so impervious to insult, so she spoke mildly, incuriously.

"Well, I put out thirty thousand midiskirts last fall, so I'm not the money or the brains. Just call me a foot soldier." Sam liked that evasion, and felt his poise returning. He wanted to do something to Betsy right then, something not carnal, like rub her exquisite shoulders until she was warm again, or waltz with her.

Harry arrived with two large drinks and gave one to Sam, who sipped lightly and put the glass on a flagstone near his feet. He was restored now, and didn't need a drink, and he worried it would ruin his day.

"Sam was just telling me about your new company," Betsy said.

"Oh, mind your own business," Harry said pleasantly.

"At least you could have asked if I wanted a drink." Betsy picked up her curious glass and started back toward the house. She was punishing Sam, for telling her nothing, by absenting herself from him.

"Pain in the ass sometimes," Harry said. "Tell me, Sam. Should I ask you how the hell you got hold of somebody else's car?"

"I'd rather you didn't," Sam said. The golden girl was gone and he was sick with loss.

"All right. But I'll tell you something that perhaps I shouldn't," Harry said. "Until this morning I was thinking of skipping town until the stupid episode blew over. That rehearsal this morning convinced me to stick around."

"Carmody knows what he's doing," Sam said. "He inspires confidence." And Sam thought how nice it would be if Price skipped town and stayed skipped, and he, Sam Deitsch, could comfort the abandoned.

When she heard the cars in the driveway, leaving, Brady Campbell went out the porch door and along a path the children had made through the woods. She stopped at the edge of the clearing and watched the cottage until she was sure nobody was inside, then crossed the bumpy, ill-cut lawn to the cottage door.

Inside was an odd mess. The furniture had been moved around

in a most unliveable way, and her hands itched to move it back to sensible order, but she was not supposed to have been there. Sandy had asked for privacy.

There was a big new table over almost against the wall for some reason, and on the table were an electric typewriter and a dicta-phone and a copying machine. Strange for a cottage, of course, but common to offices, which this cottage was supposed to be. She went into the bathroom (unaware it was a bank vault) and looked around, and she went into the bunk room and saw nothing un-usual, and she came out to the living room-kitchen, and there was nothing remarkable. Fortunately for absolutely everybody con-cerned, she did not look into the closet in the bunk room, because it had rifles and ammunition in it, and ski masks and sneakers and gloves and funny hats. But there was no reason for her to look there.

Brady became, if anything, indecently furtive leaving the cot-tage. It had all been Joanna Deitsch's idea to snoop, Joanna eaten away with curiosity about her husband's new venture. Brady ran to the shelter of the path, hurried down the path to the cover of bushes near the house, and ran again to the porch, shutting the door swiftly, firmly, behind her. Dear God! it would have been embarrassing to have Sandy come back and find her snooping. Or all of them! Brady's face flushed so she put her hands to her cheeks to cool them.

And all that at Joanna's prompting. And all that only to discover that grown businessmen were engaged in grown men's business, with typewriters and telephones with buttons. She promised herself solemnly she would not go out to the cottage again unless Sandy took her by the hand and led her.

9

Man Here Seizes Power

FOR SOME RECENT MONTHS Sam Deitsch had gotten up early, before his children, in order not to miss any worrying time. He had had so much to worry about that he welcomed Daylight Saving Time, which gave him more sun to worry under. But Four Talents had put money in his pocket, not much but all of it cash, and Sam was discovering that troubles simply did not loom in the face of hard cash. Wednesday morning he slept late for the first time in months. Inner alarms several times woke him, but he silenced them. He owned the house and he could feed everybody, and beyond that what really was there worth waking up to worry about? A robbery he must commit and his son Jerry. Sam reasoned only time could alter either, and reasoned himself back to sleep.

A flurry of bright sounds at the back door, Joanna getting Susan and Lori and Lisa off to the school bus, woke him at eight-fifteen. He smiled fondly, his eyes closed, at the pleasure of such delicious daughters and at his own great physical comfort, and drifted off again to sleep. Joanna woke him getting into bed. She slid down beside him so that her nightgown rode up to her waist, and put a chill leg across him and cold hands on him. Sam responded slowly. At night he was lover, and in the mornings Joanna took charge. When they were alone afternoons, and loving was possible, there was no telling who would make love to whom. It made for different attitudes and practices and kept them busier, and fonder, than they might otherwise have been.

Joanna made Sam very strong, and mounted him, and brought her bosom down to him. He was a little early for her, which happened mornings, but he was still strong, and Joanna went gusting off, and they lay together joined for a time, then parted and slept.

Sam woke irredeemably at nine-oh-five. Something shocked him from, and beyond contemplation of, sleep. Jerry. But why Jerry? He had lost a year's sleep over Jerry to no avail whatever. Oh, here it is. Because he might see his son this afternoon in Greenwich, and he had not told Joanna. He felt curiously unfaithful, not telling her, but he could not, there was no choice. The principal casualty thus far of the Four Talents affair was the deep intimacy between Sam and his wife. He longed, almost physically lusted, to sit quietly on the bed and wake Joanna gently and tell her all about the queer mess he had gotten into. To dissipate the longing before he succumbed to it, Sam grabbed clothes from the closet and went to the kitchen to dress.

After cereal and coffee, Sam went out back to saw logs for his four fireplaces. Sawing logs was his hobby, his sport. What tennis, golf, skiing, fishing, and hunting were to other men, sawing fireplace logs was to Sam. He had had no free time growing up, and now had no concept of leisure. He might have taken up tennis or golf if after all the effort he had something of value he could touch (present to Joanna?), and he had enjoyed fishing until one long Sunday when he had caught nothing, and he had fished only rarely since. His attitude toward leisure was best reflected in his clothes. He wore the pants of old business suits and run-down dress shoes and formerly-good button-down shirts. He had "leisure" leisure clothes by the drawerful, given him each Christmas by Joanna and the girls, fawn slacks and orange scarves and Hush Puppies and polo shirts with alligators on them that his nipples showed through. Sam wore them Christmas week to make everybody happy, feeling not unmanly but frivolous, irresponsible. Nothing in his life had prepared him for frivolity.

While he had never worked at manual labor, Sam had the gifts of strength and stamina, and he attacked his collection of fallen limbs and felled trees with his treasured bucksaw and in an hour he had enough logs for a bad December. He had also worked up a fine purging sweat in the morning sun. He stored the logs under a canvas sheet and went inside and drank cold ginger ale from the bottle, gasping and burping desperately. After a long shower, drying himself before the bathroom mirror, he frankly admired his well-used young-man's body. Bald, maybe, or getting there, and a Jew for sure, but not fat by any means, and never did smoke cigars. So much for you, Betsy Price.

Jack Carmody ate a peanut-butter-and-jelly sandwich with a large glass of milk. He wanted specifically *not* to drink until he had somebody else's car secure behind the Campbell cottage, and he had learned at AA that one way to curb the desire for a drink was a peanut-butter-and-jelly sandwich and a glass of milk. He wanted earnestly not to drink because the procurement of a hot car was exactly that piece of the Vista bank action over which he had no control, and in which his skill and courage could not compensate for the failures of others. If they faltered in the days ahead, he could lower the level of manners and press them on. If they lost heart in the bank, he had enough heart to see them out. Those were aspects of war, at which he excelled. But the theft of a car was a criminal endeavor, and he lacked skill, knowledge, and stomach for crime, so he sacrificed his midday drinks to clarity. When the car was safe behind the cottage, it would all be war again, and he would be in charge, and could permit himself several large drinks.

Although no precise time had been set, when Sam Deitsch arrived at two, it seemed sort of cavalier and sloppy to Carmody. He went out to meet the car. "Where the hell have you been?" he growled.

Mildly surprised, Sam said, "We have an hour, maybe more. What's the hurry?"

Carmody did not know what the hurry was. He had been thinking vaguely of reconnoitering the area and counting the policemen. He got into the front seat. "Well, let's go, then."

They drove north to the parkway and west toward Greenwich in silence, Sam quiet in a kind of awe at Carmody's presence, and Carmody not knowing what statement to make first, or what question to ask. At length he said, "Jerry arrange the car?"

"Yes. Jerry."

"How did he . . . ? Does he have . . . ?" Carmody did not know the next question.

"He stole a car as a prank, when he was about sixteen. Then it got to be a hobby. I had to buy him out of a dozen scrapes with the law. Maybe I should have let the police have him then. I don't know."

"What's he doing now? Just cars all the time?"

"What's he doing now," Sam said, very down. "I'll tell you what he's doing now. He's an outlaw, is what he's doing now. An outlaw. He's a pusher, a thief, a motorcycle tough living with swine in filth in the East Village. He's no good now and he never will be."

Carmody watched the road and said nothing.

"You have two boys and they're both fine sons, if I may say so. All-Americas."

"Thanks." Carmody knew what was coming, had heard it many times, and in his impatience he overheard.

"How could it happen you have two straight-arrow Galahads

when you're all the time falling down drunk chasing every broad in New York and never home or working, and I have a couple of drinks on my birthday if there's a party and I'm home every night of my marriage if I have to hitchhike and my first-born hope of heaven is an outlaw pusher?" Sam's speech was much longer than that.

"I don't know, Sam," Carmody said, because he truly didn't know. "I did a lot of things with my boys—drunk or sober—played football with them, took them fishing a lot, sailing."

"I played catch with Jerry once. Baseball. But I was just home from the office, in a suit. It was twilight and I couldn't see very well. . . . Forget it. That isn't it, anyway."

"What do you think it is?" Carmody asked gently.

Sam drummed his fist lightly on the steering wheel. "Jerry. Jerry doesn't want any part of what I am. He never wanted to be*come* what I was, or I am. Simple as that, if you get right down to it. So he makes somebody else for him to be, to become. And that somebody else is everything I am not—lazy, cruel, a bum, a thief, a tough . . ."

"That makes sense," Carmody said. "Won't make you any happier, but it makes pretty good sense." He wondered briefly who his sons had wanted to become, and he decided they had wanted to become him, their father, sober.

"I've had a lot of time to think about it," Sam said.

They left the parkway at a Greenwich exit. Sam drove knowledgeably, confidently, to the center of town. "You drive very well," Carmody said, which made Sam feel unaccountably marvelous. They parked before a dress shop opposite the train station. Sam got out, put a dime in the meter, scanned the parking lot before the station briefly, and came back into the car. "Two-thirty," he said.

"Half an hour," Carmody said. "I wonder if we should get out and look around or just sit here until we see somebody." A police patrol car went by at traffic speed, the cop looking for nothing.

There was a liquor store three doors up the street. "Let's get out and stretch our legs, anyway. We look like a stake-out or something, sitting here together."

Carmody got out. Sam locked the car and he got out too. "So they can't steal it and drive back to the City," he explained, and they both laughed.

They stretched their legs past the liquor store to an automotive supply store, where Carmody watched the parking lot in the guise of inspecting batteries and tires. "It might help if I knew just what the hell we were looking for," he said.

"Oh, you'll know them all right when they come. Probably two cars, or a car and a motorcycle. The kids will be in black leather with beards and long hair. The whole bit," Sam said with a sigh. "You'll know them."

"Let's walk back this way," Carmody said. They walked back toward the car. "Quick. In here," he said, and they ducked into the liquor store. The peanut-butter-and-jelly sandwich had worn off.

"What is it!" Sam whispered.

Carmody took a deep breath. "Nothing. Just nervous." He went to the counter and said to the clerk, "A pint of Dewar's, please," and paid, and pocketed the pint. He looked out the windows toward the parking lot. "Can't see from here," he said. "Let's get back to the car." They walked to the car and got in and Carmody beheaded the pint without taking it from the bag. He offered the bottle to Sam. "You want some?"

"Oh, God!" Sam cried. "No!"

"A simple no thanks will do," Carmody said.

"Are you nervous?" Sam asked, surprised.

"Well, why not?" Carmody said crossly. "I have to drive a stolen car all the way to Westport. Who wouldn't be nervous?"

"I wouldn't," Sam said. "They never stop you. Want me to drive it? And you drive this one?"

"You wouldn't mind driving a hot car? On the parkway? All the way to Westport?"

"Not especially. But if you're going to drive this car, please put the bottle away."

Carmody was sorely tempted, and paused, reflecting on the nature of fears and the kinds of courage, then he took a large swallow of scotch. "No. Thanks anyway, but it's not for you to do. I'll manage."

"The offer doesn't stand beyond like half a pint."

"Fair enough." Carmody took another drink. "I'll drive whatever they bring to where it's got to go."

They sat without speaking for what seemed a long time, then Sam reached down and started the car. "Here they come," he said, looking in his mirror. Carmody turned and saw a white vintage Pontiac convertible followed by a stunning brute steed of a motorcycle. The Pontiac entered the lot and joined inconspicuously the ranks of commuters' cars parked there. The motorcycle pulled up alongside the driver, and the cyclist and the driver talked. Sam pulled out into the flow of traffic, eased the car gradually right, and turned into the lot at a farther entrance. He drove calmly in a great arc and parked forty feet behind the hot car and the bike. He studied the two young men very hard and hopefully, then shrugged his shoulders mightily. "You got the money?" he said.

Carmody held up an envelope. "Right here," he said. "Doesn't look like either one of them's Jerry."

"No," Sam said. "Neither one of them's Jerry."

"Well, I'll see you around," Carmody said. He got out of the Cadillac and walked across the hot concrete to the passenger side of the Pontiac. He opened the door and got in. The motorcyclist took off his helmet and put his head in the driver's window. "You Jerry's friends?" Carmody said.

"You got the bread?" the driver said.

Carmody handed him the envelope. "Count it," he said.

"I will." Above and below his beard were rich purple acne pustules. His hair hung in long clean waves. The boy on the motorcycle watched Carmody with alert narrow eyes. Without special animosity, Carmody had an urge to smash them, to do them some wicked violence. "Two hundred," the boy said. He put the envelope in his jacket pocket and got out of the car. "There's the keys. Registration's in the dash, with the guy's license. See you around."

"So long," Carmody said. He turned the key and the car started, the engine humming smoothly. The boy who had been driving got on the back of the motorcycle and they idled clear of the cars, then gunned, roaring and careening, around the lot to the exit, and out.

On the theory that the young rat bastards had made all that noise to attract police to him, Carmody shut the Pontiac off and went back to Sam. "You follow me. I'll go straight back to Campbell's. After the noise dies down."

"That was my son's bike," Sam said distantly, aware it was neither here nor there. "You're shaking. You all right?"

"I'm fine. I had a sudden terrific desire to smash them. Both of them." He held up his trembling hands. "I damn near did. Let me have that bottle."

Sam handed out the pint. "I'll drive if you want."

Carmody seemed about to say "Oh, shut up," but he didn't. He went back to the Pontiac and drove the longest eighteen miles of his life.

Thursday morning they had to simulate the bank guard, and the person in the conference room, and Hayden the manager, because Sandy, their enduring spearholder, had taken somebody else's car out for a shakedown drive. The first rehearsal was loose and automatic, but on the second they got the numbers wrong, and by the fifth nobody, not even Carmody, got anything right. Harry Price called a break. He took off his gloves and loosened his new blue windbreaker. They were not wearing ski masks or hats, but everybody had a windbreaker shell on. "Goddamned gun gets heavy after a while," Price said.

"That's a carbine!!" Carmody said. "It's the lightest weapon we *got!* It's for typists!"

"I can't type, either. I established that early on," Price said.

"So you did," Carmody said wearily. "Now let's sit down and rest a spell and talk the thing through. Sam, you're eight. I come through the door first . . ." Sandy Campbell came through the door unannounced, and Carmody pointed his rifle right at his navel. "Sandy," he said. "Would you please knock?" He lowered his gun.

"Zero to eighty in ten seconds," Sandy said, overlooking Carmody's gun. "That car's red hot!"

"Formerly owned by a paraplegic clergyman," Price said. "Used it only to listen to the radio."

"Do you accept out-of-town checks?" Sam said.

Everybody laughed but Carmody. He was thinking several things: that it was time to lower the level of manners and treat them like green troops, which they were; that it was time to work toward one solid rehearsal, one errorless take; that it was about time to use them, put them to work, before they got any giddier. Perhaps very soon.

"I'm glad you liked the car." Carmody stood up splay-legged, the carbine dwarfed in his great hands, signaling an end to nonsense. "We missed you, Sandy. We had three-four run-throughs and nothing went right." He went to the door and put his back against it. "Now. One time. Do everything right once and we're quits. Sandy, you be the guard."

"Oh, Christ," Sandy said, but he went to be the guard. Let command who could command. "Over here?"

It did not go well. Deitsch and Price became alarmingly inept, and with each misstep Carmody got louder and meaner, shouting "Now! Now! Pick 'em up! Think! Move!" They moved. He was a frightening physical force, swinging the carbine around like a matchstick, in an apparent fury, nobody knowing if his rifle were loaded or he quite sane. The drill lasted two thoroughly unpleasant hours, and at the end of it three men hated Carmody, and he knew it. He wrapped his gun and gloves, his mask and hat, in his blue shell jacket and started for the bunk room. "That'll do for now," he said.

"Must be time for a drink," Price said, and a chill, scared silence fell. Carmody heard, but his step did not falter. He went to the bunk room and stored his gear in the closet.

"Well, it's time for lunch, anyway," Sandy said to ease the hostile quiet. "Anybody for Carpano's?"

Harry and Sam were for Carpano's all right. They brightened like reprieved lifers. Carmody appeared in the bunk room doorway. "You go ahead to Carpano's. Have a nice lunch." He looked at them without apparent recognition. "We're going in tomorrow."

"To the bank?" Sandy said. He knew where they were going in tomorrow, but he learned things best in pieces.

"Yeah. The bank." Carmody brushed at his eyes. He looked like a very tired stranger.

"What's the matter with Monday?" Sam cried.

"Tomorrow's my birthday!" Price said. (It was not.)

Carmody smiled like nobody you'd want to meet. "You're all ready. The car's all ready. I'm all ready. The bank is as ready as it'll ever be. We'll go in tomorrow." He crossed the room to the outer door amid a bristling silence. "There are no questions," he said decisively. "See you all here at eight tomorrow morning."

"What about Carpano's?" Sandy said, as Carmody was going out the door.

"You men have lunch together. Talk about women or something and not too loud. See you all here tomorrow at eight." He left.

Campbell and Price and Deitsch looked at each other like boys who had expected punishment but had escaped with only a reprimand. "I really don't like that man," Harry Price said.

Sam laughed. "You're not supposed to right now," he said. "Now about this lunch. I think I might have a little party for myself. Is there a bar around here where they let you sing in the afternoon?"

10

A Walk in the Sun

"W h o b e l o n g s t o t h a t old convertible I saw you driving this morning?" Brady asked. She was preparing to shower.

Sandy lay fully dressed on the bed, recovering from lunch. "That's the company car," he said. "For errands."

Brady put on a robe and finished undressing beneath it. "I should think you had enough cars between the four of you. Anyway, when I saw it I was a little scared what you were going to do with it."

"Scared?" Sandy was trying to keep a light fixture steady by closing one eye, but still he felt a tug of alarm. "Scared of what?"

"Well, I was afraid. . . . That isn't the car you were going to buy for young Sandy, is it?"

"Oh." The light fixture wandered away, and to hell with it. "No. That's strictly for errands. I think I can get Sandy a decent car next week."

"Good. I was afraid you were getting him a sporty old convertible, and he's not that type at all." She started for the bath-room.

"I know he's not." Brady was gone. "I wish he were." Sandy shut his eyes. *Tomorrow morning. I can't believe it. Tomorrow morning.*

Curiosity fed on Joanna's vitals. He had a new business he would not discuss and cash in his pockets he would not say where he got. He moped in front of the television, watching everything and nothing, for hours every night and had snarled at her for the first time since the Giants moved to San Francisco. Yet of all things he had taken to sleeping late some mornings, as though he hadn't a worry in the world. It was all Joanna could endure to be patient, knowing that if she were patient and didn't pry, it would all pour out of him in a boyish cry some night, and also knowing that if she sat him down and said "Something's wrong, tell me," he might shut up for good.

But patience was hard coming, because her Sam was drunk in the afternoon, singing in the downstairs playroom with their daughters, which God knows what the girls thought of their father. Give it another day, another two days if you possibly can. Patience is a virtue and O God I wish I had it.

"You didn't invest my good money in this wildcat promotion, did you?" Betsy said. It was late cocktails and she was turning surly.

"No. It's in the bank. In a special account." Harry smiled at her from the fine elevation of his renewed confidence. It was bitch time, but she couldn't hurt him anymore, and it drove her bananas.

"That wasn't a gift, you know. You were supposed to put up ten grand to match it. It was an investment."

"Monday the latest, baby. Monday the latest." How could such a pretty child be so contrary?

"Well, let's set a deadline for Monday, then." Betsy was stiff.

"I mean you get it up by Monday or you gimme back my money, right?"

"Monday it is, Betsy-love," Harry said, and any reservation he might have had about the Vista bank, and all thoughts of flight or of backing out at the last minute, evaporated. He was going in, and going in strong, and he was coming out with a bagful of money and his independence, his future.

He had been like this when they first married, right after the War, brooding, taciturn, dangerous. They might be at breakfast or a late party, and suddenly he would close himself off, lost in visions of fighting and death. Helen had tried at first to share the visions, tried to get him to talk about war, but his stories had wallowed and drowned in her incomprehension. She had not lived four months in the mud with Chappie Anderson and could not share or even imagine the horror and fear at his death, or the almost sacrificial rage that followed. She had stopped trying to get him to talk.

The brooding fits diminished and almost disappeared with the passing of time, and Helen missed them in a way. They reminded her of early marriage, a time of physical excitement, and of great change and hope. They had lived on Army posts across the south—Bragg, Sill, Bliss—while Jack considered making the Army his career, and Helen recalled the time as one long Officers' Club dance, with loving late. The early days of any marriage, bad or good, make an unerasable impress, for better or worse, and now, almost twenty-five years later, their rare loving talk was in modified southern dialect.

Jack sat now at the kitchen table, watching raw whisky over ice in a short glass, brooding. The sight of him lost in black thought woke something in Helen that had been too long asleep. She had put the dishes away and was going off to bed and it was time somehow to say something, so she asked, timidly, "Y'all comin' inta baid?"

Carmody came out of his glum and savage reverie and laughed happily in her face. "Git on in change, honey," he said. He toasted her. "I'll be raht wi'ya." He drank. "Keep yore motah runnin'."

The Campbell cottage was in a small clearing in an evergreen wood that still held the morning fog. It was a bland grey clapboard structure with many windows in white trim and a small galvanized chimney coming out of the roof. Inside it, three men of substance and accomplishments laced on basketball shoes and put on identical blue windbreaker shells, while a fourth man of strong physical presence loaded thirty-caliber carbine rifles with twenty-round clips. He, the fourth man, also a citizen of considerable merit, laid the carbines in an orderly row on the kitchen counter. "I don't want to say Fall In," he said. "It's late to be giving orders. But when you've got your sneakers and jackets on, kind of line up over there. We'll go over the gear."

The four men gathered in the center of the larger room, the living room, where furniture was strangely and innospitably disposed. Each held a shopping bag by the paper handles. On the sides of the bags an antiseptic, cute, cartoon woman purportedly said, "It's IGA for VALUE!" At a moderately phrased request from the fourth man, the other three produced from their shopping bags gloves, ski masks, and mad 1940 hats. The fourth man, seeming much the largest because he was clearly leader, took a carbine from the counter, opened and closed the bolt, and handed it to a handsome tanned man with tight grey curls. "This is yours, Harry. It's not loaded."

"It should be loaded. I'm responsible, too," Harry said. "I'd just as soon."

"That's good," Carmody said, "but you've never fired it and it's too late to learn now. Here's yours, Sam. Twenty rounds. Put a round in the chamber before we go in."

"Okay," Sam said. He removed the clip and inspected the bolt and otherwise handled the weapon familiarly before stowing it in his shopping bag.

"You take this one, Sandy. Keep it on the front seat or on the floor beside you. Out of sight, anyway. Use it with discretion. Use it with a lot of discretion."

"If at all."

Carmody looked at his watch. "Eight-forty," he said. "Let's go get us a car to ride in."

They left the cottage single file, Sandy Campbell leading, and walked around to the rear of the cottage, where a great green vinyl tarpaulin bulged with automobile. In orderly fashion they removed the tarpaulin and folded it lengthwise in fours, so it could recover the car in moments when they returned. The car was a 1965 Pontiac convertible, creamy white, with a damaged right front fender. Sandy got in behind the wheel and started the car and raced the engine lightly. "She's a sweetheart," he said. "Get around front. I'll pick you up there." Carmody and Price and Deitsch walked around the cottage to the front, the car following, bubbling idly. "Get my stuff, too," Sandy called softly as the men went back inside.

They came out of the cottage, Price holding two bags of gear. Carmody got in front and Price and Deitsch in the back. Sandy drove down his driveway and stopped at his mailbox. "It's nine-point-one miles from here," he said, and drove off.

"Who asked you how far it was?"

"Slow down."

"Stay in your bloody lane."

Alerted thus to his piss-ant role in a major, albeit amateur, criminal act, Sandy drove fast toward Vista.

"I wish to say, at this point and in all deference to our leader," Harry Price said, "that this driver chap is driving much too fast, and while I am perfectly willing to lose my life in pursuit of my fortune, I absolutely refuse to die in a shabby automobile crash."

"Slow down, Sandy," Carmody said. "You'll screw our timing."

Sandy slowed. Sam said, "You know, my brother-in-law, Milton, doesn't have the brains for a headache, he has a wife Judy with these long legs I can't describe. So Milton didn't go for midis last season and now he has money, cash, lots of it. My wife has been after me to borrow from Milton, so let me off at the corner." Sam had his thumbnail in the breech of his rifle and was inspecting the bore.

"If we pass an airport on the way, drop me off," Price said. "I'm due on the Coast for lunch." He was mashing his gloves for softness and flexibility, the better to pick up money.

"Oh, shut up and let the man drive," Carmody said.

Sam Deitsch put his carbine back in the bag and turned to Harry Price. "All over the road," he said. "And me, I haven't had a moving violation in twenty years."

"I had a father-in-law drove like this, two wives ago," Price said. "But the poor sonofabitch was sort of late spastic."

"All right. Okay," Sandy said furiously at the windshield. "But don't forget any police show up I've got to shoot it out with them."

"You men know why Sandy isn't going in, so knock it off," Carmody said mildly. "And you, Sandy. Don't get sore. Anyway, don't shoot any cops. Under any circumstances."

"I know," Sandy said with an immense sigh. "But make them stop bugging me. I have my duties and I have a function and without me—"

"You're right," Carmody said. He turned to the back. "We all have a job to do today, and Sandy's doing his right now. So let him alone." He collapsed his face in an enormous leathery wink, and turned front.

They arrived at the Vista Plaza, and entered the parking lot, and Sandy drove to the big stanchion with four great lights, near the A & P. "Open your bags between your knees," Carmody said softly, doing so himself. "Put on your gloves." They put on gloves. "Fine. Put on your ski masks." Everybody put on masks. "Hats,"

Carmody said, and they all put on hats. "Sam, put a round in your chamber." Carmody put a round in the chamber of his rifle.

"Sam," Sam said. "I'm Eight."

"Eight," Carmody said quietly. "Sorry, Eight."

Sandy drove the car directly at the bank and stopped forty feet before it. No cars. He drove on in and parked near the front door. There was a moment of great inspiration, not that of gifts but the sucking in of air common to high comedy or tragedy. "Good luck," Sandy said.

"Out," Carmody said softly. The three men, masked and in comic hats, got out of the car. They walked to the glass doors of the Vista bank, their shopping bags bumping their ankles. Going through the door, Price and Deitsch hid behind Carmody, trying to be small, or to disappear. The three entered invisibly to the degree that there was no audible alarm.

Carmody stumbled down an inside granite step he had not been told was there, and his momentum carried him to the guard in a sideways stagger rather like an Arab begging. "Good morning," he said cheerfully, not to frighten the man. He took his carbine from the shopping bag and pointed it at the guard. "Give me your gun." The guard looked up with a broad bright smile, vaguely conspiratorial, a drinking-buddy smile. Carmody took his pistol from its holster. "Get over behind the counter," Carmody said pleasantly to the guard, and the old man left. Then just as loudly as calling his battalion to attention, Carmody shouted, "*Don't muss a moovle!*" He coughed. "Don't move a muscle! This is a holdup! Seven! Eight! Let's go!"

Deitsch and Price swept around him, moving in a perfectly familiar territory they had not seen before. Eight backed the tellers to the far wall and went to clear the conference room. Seven went directly at the manager, who had his hands already locked behind his neck, and drove him off to join the tellers at the wall. Eight announced the conference room was empty, then Seven and Eight went behind the tellers' cages and started scooping money into their bags. Seven halted in the process of grabbing and stuffing money. "Wait!" he called harshly.

"What's the matter?" Eight said.

"I spill more than this! Where's all the money?" Seven waved his carbine at the rank of frightened tellers. "Whose cage is this!"

A plump girl with glasses came forward with her hands up. "I am, sir," she said, quaking.

"Then get in here and get the money up. There's more than this!"

The girl entered her cage, and trembling so badly she could scarcely manipulate, opened the bottom drawer of a filing cabinet, divulging great sums in bundles. "Here, sir," she said, and stepped back to the comfort of numbers. Harry jammed the big bundles into his bag. "Okay, okay! Splendid!" he boomed. "Who's got the next cage?"

Another woman, pinch-faced, hostile, and Irish, came forward. "I knew they'd be around," she said. "That's why I told 'em hide the money."

"Shut up and make me some money!"

"Yes, sir." She found some small keys and opened the lower drawer of her filing cabinet. Large bundles of money came to view. "Thank you," Price said, stuffing money in his bag. "Next!" A pretty and timid girl came gracefully forward and with a hint almost of flirtation uncovered her reserve cash from beneath a counter. She withdrew.

Through all this Carmody had adopted a straddle-legged Colossus of Rhodes posture in mid-floor, watching with a sort of encouraged dismay as all plans and rehearsals went for naught. Then he saw a small bald man with a mop emerge from behind the steel vault (bathroom) door to see what was going on. "Seven! Eight!" Carmody shouted. "The vault!"

Eight ran to the vault and jammed the barrel of his carbine in it, so it could not be shut. Seven put his rifle muzzle under the recently barbered chin of Malcolm Hayden. "Any money in there?" he asked, gesturing with his shopping bag at the vault.

"Lots," Hayden said. He had been prepared to be brave, but he was married now.

"Then help us get it out," Seven said. Hayden, hands behind his neck, went to the vault and indicated, by nodding his pompadour nervously, where money might be found. Seven rested, his gun on Hayden, while Eight cleared the money into his bag. Eight then ran out to Six, in the center of the bank floor. "You were very wise," Seven said to Hayden. "Now join the others, please."

"Yessir," Hayden said, and left, hands still clasped behind his neck.

Seven and Eight, Harry and Sam, wove behind Carmody and out the door, to the car. Carmody backed to the door and held there, a figure of grand menace. "First face out the door gets blown off!" he announced commandingly. He opened the door, stepped out, and ran to the car.

When Carmody was aboard, Sandy whipped the car around and raced off. Carmody grabbed his shoulder and lifted him almost clear of the seat. "Slow down!" he said harshly. "Get rid of the hats and ski masks now! Quick!" Carmody said, taking his off. "Put them in your bags. Take off the shells and put them in too."

"Help me with this thing," Sandy said, struggling with his ski mask. "I can't see."

"Slow down," Carmody said, helping him with the mask. "Somebody take this man's gear." He thrust Sandy's hat and mask rearward. "Now slow down, will you? We're clear."

They proceeded then at a most comfortable pace to the Campbell home, and up the driveway to a small cottage, and parked immediately to the rear of the cottage. The four men quickly covered the car with the great vinyl tarpaulin and trooped in a body around front and into the cottage, bearing "I buy IGA for VALUE!" bags. They put the bags together in the center of the floor and stood about directionless. It was a part of the operation they had not rehearsed.

"Into the bunk room," Carmody said wearily. "Put the whole bloody mess in the closet." They did so, in a sort of eager crush, and came out again to the living room, where they looked at one another and began laughing, great manly shouts of laughter, in an ecstasy of relief. It had been so easy. A piece of cake. A walk in the sun.

Sam stopped laughing first and rushed for the bathroom. Harry Price was suddenly consumed by shakes, his shoulders and knees quaking, even his ears visibly trembling. Carmody went to the cabinet and rewarded himself with a strong drink. "All right, Sandy," he said. "You're in charge again now. The offensive action is over, and I abdicate. Christ, man," he said to Harry. "Look at you shake! Have a drink." He brought a glass of whisky to Price and held it to his white lips. Harry drank.

"Harry here saved our ass in the bank," Carmody said. "All credit, full marks, to Harry Price! Drink up, man."

"Harry saved you? What happened?" Sandy asked.

"He and Sam were cleaning out the tellers' stations while I covered everybody and Harry realized we weren't getting much money. 'I spill more than this,' he yelled." Carmody laughed. "So he hustled the tellers over and we got at the real money, under the counters. Steady, man. Don't gulp. Let me get some more." Carmody, earnestly protective, got more whisky and put a little water on top of it and took it to Price and hand-fed him slowly. "Easy. Don't gulp. Then a janitor with a mop sticks his head out of the vault and Harry—would you believe it?—puts that empty gun under the manager's chin and forces him into the vault to help fill the bags with more money.

"There. That's enough for now. I always thought it took a lot of balls to stand up on live television before a surly nation, and you got a lot of balls. Do you always shake like this?"

"After every performance of my life," Harry said.

"Jesus. I wonder is it worth it?"

"I've often wondered myself. Thank you for the help. I can hold the glass now by myself."

Sam emerged from the bathroom looking dimly shamed. "Sorry," he said. "I couldn't go. For three–four days I was too nervous."

"You did look a little green," Carmody said. "Sandy, what's next? I don't want to give orders any more. I make enemies."

Sandy shrugged. "Split up. Go home. Forget about it. I'll count the money and deduct the expenses and figure the shares. Then I'll call you."

That was sensible, and the end of it, and there was no disagreement, but still nobody moved. They had been together, working toward a fearful climax, for ten days, and now the climax was behind them, and they were reluctant to part. "Before you deduct the expenses," Carmody said, "why don't you include the cost of a small, smart gala at the Club for Four Talents and their wives?"

"I think that's a splendid idea," Harry Price said. "Cocktails and dinner, the wine flowing like water . . ."

"And dancing," Sam added. He still wanted to waltz or something with Betsy Price.

After a moment's hesitation (he was in charge again), Sandy said, "I don't see why not, if nobody gets drunk and talks a lot. Saturday night at the Club. Definitely. I'll have Brady call your wives. . . .

"Now I can see you're all reluctant to split up, and I understand it because I'm sorry to see you go, but we've got to separate. Shake hands all around. Leave at, say, five-minute intervals." They shook hands. Price left first, followed by Sam Deitsch. Carmody stayed to the last, as usual, finishing a drink. Sandy said, "Just like you said, Jack. A walk in the sun."

"We're not out of it yet," Carmody said. "That was the easy

part." He drained his glass and put it on the stove. In the face of the absurdity of their recent undertaking, and its unlikely success, they were at a loss for words. "My best to Brady and the kids," Carmody said.

"My best to Helen and the boys," Sandy said. Carmody left.

11

The Private Lives
of Underworld Figures

As they discovered in later conversations, three of the four principals in the robbery resisted only with effort and luck the impulse to return to the Vista Plaza and see what furor they had wrought. Sam Deitsch had in fact made three decisive turns toward Vista when the music on his radio stopped.

"We interrupt our scheduled program to bring you this news bulletin," an announcer said gravely. Sam noted it was 10:10, an hour exactly since they had entered the bank.

"The Vista, New York, branch of the Westchester County Trust Company was held up this morning by a gang of masked men armed with shotguns. There were no injuries, and the gunmen fled with an estimated sixty thousand dollars. An all points alarm has been issued, covering Westchester and Fairfield Counties, and police check points have been set up on all major roads leading to New York City.

"Police said the robbery was smooth and quick, indicating the thieves were professionals. Because state lines may have been crossed in the process of the robbery, Vista police chief Frank W. Hemmings said he was appealing for help to the Federal Bureau of Investigation.

"To repeat our latest bulletin . . ." Sam turned the radio off. The FBI! J. Edgar Hoover! He slowed at the next driveway, backed and turned vigorously, and started back to Westport to tell Jo-anna. He passed Harry Price, coming the other way, but did not see him.

Price also gave in temporarily to the urge to return to the scene of the crime. He knew that criminals were supposed to return to the scene, and that police were supposed to take pictures of crowds gathered at the scene, but it was all too utterly hackneyed to be-lieve, and if the criminal returning had showed up in a script, he would have penciled it out. So he, too, made three decisive turns toward Vista, and his radio not on might surely have continued, had he not recognized Sam Deitsch's Cadillac boiling down the road at him, and seen Sam hunched furiously behind the wheel like a man escaping.

Harry turned at the next (the same) driveway and drove back to Westport and home. He suffered a strong, nameless hunger, and in his kitchen he opened the refrigerator on an absurd pleni-tude of food, which only repelled him. He was not hungry that way. The hunger began to focus as he walked toward the wing of the house he and Betsy kept for themselves, free of guests and servants. Betsy was still asleep, all warm blonde and pink lumps against red sheets. Harry's hunger was too large for a dimension, but it most certainly had now a definite focus. He undressed rapidly.

"What are you doing up?" Betsy asked sleepily.

"It's all right. Everything's all right. Don't move." Harry got in beside her.

"What time is it?"

"Early. Very early." He pulled her tight to him.

"Mercy!" Betsy said.

Jack Carmody knew that criminals always returned to the scene of the crime. He used to go to the movies. But he felt a strong pull toward Vista and might have gone back anyway, had he not become suddenly sleepy. He was at the foot of Campbell's drive and prepared to turn right toward Vista when his forehead seemed to slide down over his eyes. It was a sensation he experienced rarely but definitely, and he rooted around in his tired mind and remembered. When his battalion had finished its two-week summer shoot at Camp Drum, and the troops and artillery were safely delivered to the armory, then he felt suddenly, deathly sleepy in this way. It was relief, the end of responsibility, of command. For all the bank affair was nowhere near an end, his part, the war part, was over. From here on in it was a crime, an unlawful procedure, and somebody else could be in charge. He turned left at the end of the driveway and drove home, yawning mightily. He cooked a platter of bacon and eggs, which he ate with toast and coffee, and he lay down on his bed. Even with a pint of fresh coffee in him, he fell asleep immediately.

Carmody woke at one, feeling fresh and carefree and slightly rich. He decided to go to the Club and drum up a gentlemanly game, and let the pigeons win a few bucks for a change.

Sandy alone had no desire to return to Vista. He had, indeed, been very much afraid he would have to go back to the bank, after the robbery, and cash his unemployment check, but to his great relief the assault had been moved up to Friday, and now he had three days before he *must* return to the bank, and he was not going there until he had to.

Besides, he had a stronger desire, amounting almost to a lust, and that was to count the money. It was a profound curiosity that had nothing to do with greed. How much do bank robbers make?

For just what kind of money had four worthy citizens risked so very much?

His approach was orderly and unhurried. He took the three bags with money from the closet and emptied them on an upper bunk, then replaced the carbines and other paraphernalia, and returned the bags to the closet. The money covered much of the bunk bed in a disarray that was entirely satisfying, and which he set about deliberately to order. First he put all the loose bills in one heap and all the bundled bills in another. Then, like a rich madman playing solitaire, he laid bills down in descending order of value, stacking money according to denomination. When this was done, he gave a slight start and pulled the shade closed on the bunk room window, then went to the front door of the cottage and locked it from the inside. He took a manila pad and a ballpoint pen from the table in the living room and put them at the top of the bunk, where the pillow belonged. On the left, as he faced the money, was a solitary neatly bound package of crisp bills, the paper wrapper reading $100. He counted the bills three times, and entered on the manila pad, with great satisfaction,

> 100's   100 at $100 each $10,000

He held what he had written at arm's length and admired it. What a handsome beginning!

By employing severest personal discipline, Carmody had managed to lose twelve dollars to Jim Sinclair at golf, and for the first time in years had taken no money from Bunny Hibbard. Sinclair, who had recently sold half of Waterbury for tax loss purposes, was delirious at taking twelve bucks from Jack. He called for champagne and dancing girls and feasting till dawn, but they made do with drinks and Cheese-bits at the Back Nine bar. Hibbard insisted the party was on him. Carmody smiled as Sinclair told everybody how he won, his smile thinning as each new arrival was told. At six, Sinclair asked the bartender to turn on television and Carmody, just a little testy, said, "You only took me on three holes. I don't think the networks will pick it up."

"Sorry, Jack," Sinclair said, not contrite at all. "But it will be a long time before I beat you again, so I want to make the most of it. No. I want to watch television for the news. They robbed a bank up north of here."

"Who's they?" What else to ask?

"Who? I don't know," Sinclair said. "Some gang from the City. With shotguns. Got away with sixty grand." He and Hibbard studied the set as an image formed at the close of a commercial. Carmody didn't know what was coming on the screen or how he would react to it, so he breathed carefully and kept his hands in evidence, as he did with good cards at poker.

The bank robbery was the lead story on the CBS news out of Hartford. There was a shot of the bank front with a caption reading VISTA, N.Y. beneath it. Carmody could not quite grasp the commentary. Either he was nervous deaf or he was trying too hard to hear if anybody had been arrested, or if police had any leads. The camera panned the parking lot, which was no longer empty. There had to be a hundred cars in the lot, with people out of them milling and rubbernecking. They cut to a medium shot of the manager, with a caption below him reading M. G. HAYDEN MGR. He was questioned by a reporter, whose questions Carmody could not quite hear. Nor could he hear Hayden's answers until he said "shotgun." ". . . held a shotgun under my chin and forced me into the vault. They were very quick and efficient, so I did exactly what they told me," Hayden said with a small laugh. They cut back to the studio and the announcer summed up, using the word "professional" twice. Carmody sighed bitterly through clenched teeth. They were out of it clean. He pushed his glass at the bartender. "Fix that, will you, Frank?" he said.

"Sixty thousand dollars," said Bunny Hibbard. "We're all in the wrong business."

"No," Carmody said. "It's not worth it."

Sam Deitsch bathed in a sublime element. He lay on a wide couch, entirely surrounded by daughters. Even Susan, who was too old now for cuddling, was on the couch with him, warming his leg. Lori and Lisa lay on either side of him, warmth and fragrance. Joanna had come downstairs to watch the eleven o'clock news and sat perched at the head of the couch, not to block anyone's view. Sam dozed in nectar until the announcer identified the top news stories of the day: a cabinet resignation, an airplane highjacking, a riot at Bowling Green University, a bank robbery in Vista, New York, a celebrity jewel theft, and an imminent hot spell. A bright bolt of fear struck Sam's stomach at the sound of Vista. FBI! Jail! Disgrace! Loss! Yet he could say nothing to anybody who mattered, who could ease him. "Oooo!" Joanna said. "They robbed the bank at Vista! Girls? Remember that bank? We shop there all the time," she said to Sam.

There was loud speech stopped in his throat, and Sam had a need for some kind of violent gesture. He sat up rudely. "You what!" he shouted. Lisa fell to the floor.

"We shop there. At the A & P. Everything's loss leader. It's almost free. What's the matter with you?"

"It's dangerous!" Sam cried. "They rob the bank!"

"Oh, don't be silly and help Lisa up," Joanna said. "There it is! Look!"

The Vista bank was on the screen. A voice spoke in grave, quick tones. There was a shout in Sam's throat ("I did it! Help me! FBI! Help!") that threatened to suffocate him. He might have shouted, but the picture on the screen became the Vista Plaza, and there was a sudden rush of girl and woman talk around him and the sheer noise of it calmed him. The bank manager came on the screen, and then the network announcer, and then the President, holding a piece of paper. "Oh, well," Joanna said. "Too bad."

"What's too bad?" Sam said. (You don't know how bad it is.)

"Nobody knew about the place. It was always empty. Everything was cheap. Now they robbed the bank everybody will be going there and it'll be just as expensive as everyplace else."

"That's what's too *bad!*" Sam demanded. "*That's* too bad?"

He could have screamed at her "The *troubles* I got! The trouble I'm *in!*" but instead he stared at her, his whole body bulging with information.

"Sam," Joanna said reasonably, "why are you acting crazy?"

"I'm sorry," Sam said. He lay back on the couch and pulled Lori and Lisa close to him again. What he had lost at Vista was a part of his family life: intimacy. Now he would watch and wait and see what he gained in exchange.

Like motion pictures, television carried the wrong messages to Harry Price. He became so absorbed in technique and detail that he grasped only marginally what was being conveyed. When he saw the shots of the Vista bank and the Vista Plaza on television, his immediate response was outrage at the cameraman who had been lazy enough or stupid enough to use the same lens for both shots. Not until he read the account of the robbery in *The New York Times* on Saturday morning did he have full awareness that his walk in the sun with friends had been an antisocial act that the press must decry and the police must punish.

Harry and Betsy were sitting on white wrought-iron chairs before a white wrought-iron table with a glass top on an enclosed terrace outside the semiprivate bedroom wing of their house. They breakfasted in the Continental style Betsy had acquired making a picture called "Dieppe!"—café filtre with hot cream and croissants with sweet butter. Harry finished the *Times* story of the robbery, noting with satisfaction that it was attributed to eight professionals, and he needed to talk just then, so he talked of something else. "This new company I'm in is having what they call a small smart gala tonight. Drinks, dinner, dancing, that kind of thing. At the Club. Shall we go?"

Betsy looked up from the Stamford *Item.* "Why not? I'd love to go."

"Good. Sandy's wife will probably call you. I don't know her name, but I hear she's very nice. . . ."

Betsy shrieked with sudden laughter, and just as suddenly fell silent again. She examined her paper to see if her eyes had deceived her. They had not, and she went into peals of abandoned laughter, rocking and weeping, collapsing the newspaper and dropping it to the terrace. "What the hell is it?" Harry asked, alarmed by this un-actress-like, un-Betsy-like behavior.

Between helpless shrieks of laughter, Betsy said, "They had a . . . bank robbery up . . . the street somewhere . . ." It was too much to continue.

"I read about it in the *Times*," Harry said calmly.

Betsy picked up her paper, found her page. "And one of the tellers '. . . Eileen Flynn of Lebanon Street, New Canaan, said, "I couldn't identify any of the men. They had masks on. But one of them said 'splendid' the way Harry Price, God rest his soul, used to say it on the Harry Price Theater when I was a girl. . . .' " Betsy lowered her head to her arms, laughing, and slid from her chair to the terrace, laughing.

"Let me see that goddamned paper!" Harry roared. "Where is it! What page!" He tore at the newspaper in a fury, then found the place. "Eileen . . . masks on . . . Harry Price, God rest his *soul!* God rest my *so-ul!*" He crumpled all of the paper into a small ball. "Jesus God, I'll rest *her* soul!" He slammed the paper ball down on weeping Betsy and stormed into the house to call his lawyers. "God rest my soul?" he roared. "God rest my *soul?*" Betsy lay on the terrace still, laughing helplessly.

Helen Carmody woke late, because it was Saturday, and alone, as was her custom. She bundled herself up in a robe, for although she slept alone she favored daring nightwear, and went to the kitchen, where she discovered her husband having coffee. "You're up early," she said.

"It's a nice day." Carmody lit a cigarette to wake his eyes. "Gonna be a hot one."

"Would you like breakfast?" Helen's personality was in neutral.

Events had not yet determined who she would be today, so she was her impersonal, or office, self.

"No thanks. I'll put up the awning and set up the table and chairs outside first and have a sandwich later." They had decided the night before to invite the other Talents and their wives and a few neighbors by for drinks before dinner. "Will you call Brady and the others?" Carmody said. He didn't want to put up the awning and put out the table and chairs if nobody was coming.

"I'll call her. Don't rush me. It's only ten." Helen's voice abruptly acquired a ragged edge.

"Okay. Take it easy," Carmody said. "I'll set it all up anyway." He went outside to enjoy the splendid June day, and to get out of range. If he stayed underfoot, Helen would turn into the Crazy Lady, which Carmody liked to avoid when guests were coming. He entered the house again by way of the bulkhead doors to the cellar, and brought out first an aluminum stepladder, which he set up against one of four strong beech trees that formed a square in the back lawn. Then he wrestled up the cellar stairs with a green-and-white striped awning folded into a cumbersome bundle. He pulled it to the trees and unfolded it between them so that one corner reached each tree. For an hour he moved the ladder from tree to tree, securing the awning, adjusting it, making it taut. The sun was high and hot but not yet punishing. It would be a fine beach afternoon. He brought from the cellar a table made of redwood slabs that had weathered a handsome rose-grey and set it among the trees, under the canopy. Last he brought up several summery chairs and set them at random in the shade. When he had finished, he stepped back and looked at his work with pleasure. A clean, cool place to drink. The awning and the table meant summer to him, whatever the calendar said.

Another summer. A hot June day. If either of the boys was around, they would go to the beach for the afternoon, or sailing. He had not even put his boat in the water last summer because neither of the boys was around to sail with. He missed them. Sons keep you young. For a second summer they would both be away, in Germany and at college. Carmody said aloud where his thoughts led him. "Sonofabitch," he said. "Old."

The kitchen was empty, and Carmody put ice in a short glass and poured scotch whisky and some water over the ice and set it to chill. He took a pencil from a forest of implements in a cup on the kitchen counter, and an old telephone bill from a pile of unpaid bills, and sat at the kitchen table, drink at his elbow, to write, with keen pleasure:

Split Case Quarts (12)

3 Dewar's	
3 Gordon's gin	
1 Vermouth	Ice, soda,
2 Vodka	tonic, potato
2 Junk	chips, etc.
11	

He changed "3 Dewar's" to "4 Dewar's" and changed the total to "12." A shopping list suitable for framing. Helen came furiously into the kitchen, but Carmody was too pleased with his world to notice her mood. "Did you call everybody?" he said.

Helen turned on him. "Why are you so anxious that I call everybody all of a sudden? You decide on the spur of the moment in the middle of the night to have a party . . ." Here Carmody's private ear took over. He put more whisky in his glass and started from the kitchen, hearing, "You get two fast bucks to rub together and you can't wait to make a list for booze on the back of a telephone bill that they've shut off the service anyway to feed your friends who are never there when you need them and I slave all week . . ."

Jack shut the bedroom door behind him, dimming the shrill, dismal litany. He would have money soon, and he would get an apartment in town and a small job and have lunch with friends. And there would be women. Quiet women.

He pursued and explored and enlarged his favorite fantasy. At no time did he think of the robbery. He had in his time faded a lot of terrible memories, and now he was fading the memory of Vista. Even working in the hot sun, his mind idle, he had not thought of Vista.

12

Payday

BECAUSE THERE WOULD otherwise be only one topic of conversation—a robbery, and it unmentionable—Carmody invited several neighbors to cocktails, a gesture which served to fuel the Crazy Lady, solitary and thrashing in her kitchen. Among those he invited, with an eye to ethnic balance, were the Donatellis, who accepted, and the Manchers, a new, rich, spade couple down the road, who declined for perhaps the fifth time, and fuck them. Carmody dressed in a natural linen jacket and black slacks and slip-on shoes. His shirt was button-down broadcloth he had had made by dozens in better times, with starched French cuffs, only the cuffs starched. He wore a skinny black four-in-hand tie which he tucked into a broad, tight black cummerbund. Dressed, he stood before an enormous mirror, and decided he looked marvelous. "You are a very vain man," he said aloud to the mirror, and his image nodded at him. He passed through the kitchen on the way to the side yard, ignoring Helen in her hair curlers and scullery clothes in a fashion calculated to drive her mad. One of the few joys in having a madwoman for a wife is nudging her along.

The fine weathered redwood table under the canopy was deep with glittering bottles and covered by glassware in shining ranks and tubs of ice with tongs and chips and dips and hors d'oeuvres on trays and a big silver pitcher full of a punch Carmody had concocted during his brief fling with AA, for those who elected not, or were forbidden, to drink. He felt tall and trim and perfectly smashing and took a scotch raw, then poured scotch over ice, and water from a pitcher. A cool, clean place to drink. Perhaps he could arrange with the boys to be buried near here.

The first arrivals were Sam and Joanna Deitsch, and they asked for Cokes. In the face of Carmody's evident, immediate disappointment, Sam explained he was just thirsty from the drive and would have a drink after the Coke. Joanna laughed at Carmody. A great bang issued from the house, which noise Carmody identified as Helen, working, and Joanna went at once to help. She had not gone five steps when Sam hissed, "They called in the FBI. I heard it on the radio."

"Shhh," Carmody said, pointing at Joanna. When she had reached the back steps, he said, "Then we're safe like in church. FBI hasn't caught anybody in forty years."

"That's all you got to say? That's all you got to *say!*" Sam betrayed now traces of early Delancey Street in brutish posture, in scarcely controlled anger.

Carmody looked down at Sam thoughtfully, reappraising him. "No," he said. "That's not all I got to say." Vito and Marina Donatelli had driven up and were getting out of their car. "What I got to say to you is forget it. Forget it ever happened. . . ."

"Are you crazy? Forget I walked into a bank with . . ."

"Never interrupt when I'm talking what I know." Carmody kept his voice very down. "Learn to forget. Practice forgetting. Try. Every time it comes to your mind, push it out. Push, you hear?

It will go. Trust me." He smiled and lay a gentling hand on Sam's hard, angry shoulder. "Now I want you to meet members of another belabored ethnic group. Hello, Marina. Hello, Vito. Meet Sam Deitsch. Sam is our Jew."

That was the last heard of the Vista affair until dinner, when Betsy Price, with immoderate prefatory laughter, told everybody that a bank teller in a robbery somewhere had said that one of the gunmen "said 'splendid' the way Harry Price, God rest his soul, used to say it on the Harry Price Theater when I was a girl." The story was greeted with reserved amusement, out of manners by some, and out of fright by others. Recovering quickly from abandoned laughter, Betsy decided they were a bunch of Eastern stiffs, and with the sure aim of a girl much courted asked Sam if he would dance with her. Sam sprang.

Dinner was a social triumph, the conversation, ambience, fellowship surviving what had to be called a meal. For example: Harry Price found himself between Brady Campbell, whom he could not fathom, and Joanna Deitsch, who was right there on top, take it or leave it, apparently without a secret in the world. When Sam and Betsy would not stop dancing and *would* not stop dancing, Harry asked Joanna to dance. She declined. "I'm not jealous," she said. "Good. I hate dancing," Harry said. "Would you be jealous if Sam took a mistress?" Joanna laughed at him. "That was fifteen years ago and I was mad as hell until I met her." "Then it was all right?" Harry said. "Great!" He turned to his right and asked Brady how she would feel if Sandy took a mistress, and Brady looked at him as though he were bait in a can. "Sandy," she said with incomparable disdain, "has his hands full." She excused herself and left the table without deigning to announce a destination. Harry felt her departure, and strangely, in his ribcage. "What did you say to Brady?" Joanna demanded. "Same thing I said to you. About a mistress," Harry said. "Boy are you dumb," Joanna said. "Well what the hell, you didn't mind, and I was only making conversation." Joanna looked around as if for help. "Dumb," she said. "Dum-dum-dum-dum."

Another example: Because he knew there was less likelihood of Vista talk with outsiders around, Carmody had insisted the Donatellis join them for dinner. (The Donatellis because they always had an older relative in their woodwork to babysit, and because he and Vito enjoyed each other noisily.) With all the delicacy possible to a rude temperament, Carmody told a story about an Italian family driving out to picnic, when one of the children had a messy accident in the back seat. The father pulled over to the side of the road, sniffing, stopped the car, turned menacingly to the back, and said, "All right. Which one-a-you wise sumona-bitches open-a-lunch?" Vito asked what it said on Coke bottles in Ireland. What? Open other end. And, when does an Irishman go to the poorhouse? When? In a Cadillac to visit his mother. Vito was olive, small, delicate, quick, ornamental. There was a terrible amused intelligence in his eyes. He was a man of control. Beside him Carmody looked like the Statue of Liberty with hair. They were Fat & Skinny, bumpkin and sharper, Lenny and George. They did not so much converse for the benefit of others as put on an act for an audience, whenever they could capture one. They were really very funny unless, like Marina Donatelli, you had grabbed their act maybe forty times.

Item: With Brady gone from between them, Harry tried to talk with Sandy Campbell. (Joanna, to his left, was too honest for conversation.) Sandy talked of doom on Wall Street and Harry countered with doom on the Coast, and both fell suddenly silent, listening, when a young guitarist on the bandstand started to sing *Nobody Knows You When You're Down and Out*. There passed between them then the electric and irrevocable bond of afición. "Bessie's song," Harry said, and Sandy nodded, smiling privately, listening. Long pause, the boy singing not so good, but the song! "You haven't really heard her yet," Sandy said. "Every record she ever made." "Tell you later." Sandy lifted his chin, indicating the boy with the guitar. They listened together, hereinafter insepara- bles.

Semiwindup: Helen Carmody fell asleep at the table after din- ner, to no one's surprise and with considerable propriety. In her husband's phrase, she was "alertly passed out." Betsy and Sam came back from interminable dancing, Sam aglow with a pure love, and Betsy, to whom a party was simply not a party unless it ended in a skinnydip, proposed that everybody go back to her place. That seemed a fine idea, all around. Brady had returned to the table perceptibly drunker than when she had left. "She wan- ders," Sandy explained to Harry, helping Brady to sit. "Look," he said. "Why don't you drive Brady to your place and I'll stop at home and get this Bessie record I want you to hear." "Fine," Harry said. "Brady, would you mind riding with Harry while I get the record?" "Not especially," Brady said, queenly stiff. "Well, that's just splendid of you. Splendid!" Harry boomed, with all summon- able irony.

For a gang of thieves and their molls, Price thought, they were a damned good-looking group. They sat about in a quad of couches in the center of his living room drinking stingers Carmody had shaken up from Harry's twelve-year-old Armagnac on the grounds that cheap brandy made him sneeze. That was like Carmody, the arrogance, but it was like the rest of them too. Each couple repre- sented a terrifically expensive operation—class housing, private schools, good clothes and cars, the best food and booze, clubs, churches, charities. When actors were making big money a few years ago, none of them knew where to put it—they had no back- ground in expenditure—and what didn't go to Uncle Sam went to Vegas. But these people could blow unspeakable wampum with- out going near Picasso or Cartier.

Harry was apart from the group, by his stereo, ostensibly listen- ing hard to an LP of Bessie Smith that Campbell, of all people, had actually gone home and gotten for him when they left the Club. It was, for a fact, the first time Price had really heard Bessie, his own records being crude distortions. It had been thrilling at first to hear her true clarity and lightness, but Harry had been listening a long time now, and his attention wandered. Out of old habit he began casting everybody in the room, Carmody and Betsy first because they were easiest. Jack could play any Robert Ryan role he wanted, especially the tough loner cop. He actually looked more dangerous than Ryan, although Price would never tell Ryan that to his face. Betsy was a director's dream. She could be anybody. Tell her what you wanted and point a camera at her and you had it in one take. She could be a big star if she had that raw, insane ambition, but if she were sufficiently ambitious, she would never have married Harry Price.

Sam Deitsch, curiously enough, would make a perfect gangster. He was a rock physically, which is probably where his gentleness came from. His head was a rock. His shoulders and arms were rocks. He could play any Edward G. Robinson role right now and improve on it. Funny they were both gentle men and both had kid trouble.

Sandy Campbell, unfortunately, could step right into "Father Knows Best" except for that wife of his. She was no situation-comedy helpmeet. So make him a television widower. "My Three Sons." Or take twenty pounds off him and let him do Charlton Hestons.

Sleeping Helen Carmody tomorrow could be Sam Spade's Effie or Perry Mason's Della. Also on the basis of an earlier conversation with her, she could do Charlotte Corday in a walk. Joanna Deitsch was absolutely perfect for the part of Joanna Deitsch, which had not yet been written. Harry had played his casting game for many years, and he thought very highly of people who refused to be duplicated or replaced.

That left (since the Donatellis had gone along home) Brady Campbell. She was a tough one to cast: Harry was much taken with her. She was a knockout in an odd, plain way. He wondered if the quality would hold up on film. Possibly, but you'd have to build the vehicle around her, or her quality. She wasn't traditionally pretty enough to be a traditional leading lady, and there was too much to her for second leads. The strong woman parts— *Medea, Foxes, Macbeth*—were all bitch parts, and not for her. Then he had it, so exactly right he laughed aloud, one short bark, "Ha!" *Helen of Troy. You could build a picture around Brady Campbell as Helen of Troy and use a gang of mickey-mice to support her, and nobody would notice.*

Even as he saw it, and saw how perfect it was, Harry knew he could never tell her, or much of anybody, because it was a barefaced declaration of love. Alone in a corner, listening to Bessie, he shrugged hugely. He had had dumber crushes.

Main event: Betsy could feel nudity pushing out through her clothes. The stingers were watery, Helen had seized the occasion to catch up on her sleep, and the conversation was funereal in a precise sense: there was something everybody was talking around, as one talked around the deceased at a funeral. Probably something to do with the new partnership, because it had not been mentioned all night long. Betsy was bored and nudity urged outward. "I'm going for a swim," she announced mildly, and to no one in particular. She threw off a small pink jacket and started toward the open doors to the terrace and the pool, then stopped in the doorway, her hand on the zipper high on the back of her dress. "Anybody join me?"

"Sure," said Carmody, gravely interested. He went to the door and helped Betsy with her zipper. She stepped out of her dress and tossed it on a rosebush and disappeared into the dark, Carmody following. Whatever quality of innocence that might attach to adults swimming naked at night was lost.

"Oh, Sam," Joanna said. "Go for a swim before you bust a gut." Sam was seated, yet crouched as if to spring.

"Aren't you coming?" Harry said to Joanna. He was barefoot in his trousers with his shirttails out. Brady and Sandy went out into the dark fully clothed and hand in hand, like chaperones.

"I don't want to go for a swim," Joanna said. "I'll take off my clothes so I won't spoil everything, but I don't want to swim." She got up and went to the door. "Come on, Sam. Hurry up. Jack Carmody's got your girl." Sam hurried out after her.

The pool and terrace suddenly blazed with light as Harry worked the switches. Betsy shrilled something and Harry worked more switches and the lighting was muted. He went out to the shallow, darker end of the pool and took off his shorts and dived in. In the cold calm and the dark he did an idle breast stroke, not to disturb the surface. Carmody, Betsy, solid Sam frolicked at the far end of the pool, by the board.

Brady appeared naked at poolside. She was strongly made, as if blocked out, then feminized, and seemed not tall at all without clothes. Harry floated so that only his head was above water. He was not peeping but a camera now, and a camera with an excellent angle. *Those, baby, are truly the hips that launched a thousand ships.* Brady watched the water, and for all the boistering around her only the water, then dived, an execution of great simplicity and functional beauty. "O, a hundred pounds sterling!" Harry said, aloud and quietly, to start the bidding. Sandy came fast out of the dark and launched himself without pause into the water. He frothed across the pool, made a racing turn, and drifted, face down, to the middle. After a really considerable time, he popped his head up and cried "O! This is de*lic*ious!"

It was. What was equally delicious was that Harry had taken unkind notice, as Sandy raced from the dark, that he was hung like a chipmunk. The most proper gentleman will notice that sort of thing, if he is interested in the woman. Perhaps Helen left Menelaus . . . ? No. It was all unworthy and sordid. He tried to dismiss it from his mind, but it would not dismiss, so he laughed it off, and laughing asked, Why did Helen run off with Paris, anyway? And why did Menelaus, if he was any kind of stud, take her back? Something was wrong in that house, and perhaps many-judgemented Menelaus had a joint like a pinky. If, indeed and of course, it *was* Menelaus, and not Agamemnon or Onassis or some other Greek.

Brady climbed the ladder at the far end of the pool, the muscle of her buttocks hollowing and flexing. For the first time, Harry felt like a peeper, and stood up nipple-deep in the water, to be seen. O, hips, hips! Launch this ship!

Betsy shrieked, which frantic appeal brought Harry's focus reluctantly from contemplation of Brady's sturdy feminine grace, not to say her dripping ellipsoidal ass, to the sight of Carmody holding his child bride like a child indeed. Jack stood at the end of the diving board, holding squealing Betsy out over the water, laughing. He had a mat of hair on his chest and shoulders out to Wednesday and great calves with veins in them popping. A rope of cock came down nearly to mid-thigh. A man, Harry thought. No more control than a blizzard, but a man, by Jesus.

And Harry decided it was perhaps just as well the Four Talents thing was at an end, and that perhaps it was better the Talents didn't see very much of each other socially in the future.

Payday was Sunday, at three, in the Campbell cottage. Sandy had provided a plastic container of bloody mary mix, which he touted as impenetrably curative, and gin and vodka and a bowl of ice. He and Price had a restorative drink, Sam abstaining. Carmody had a scotch-rocks-splash, not his first of the day.

"This," Sandy began portentously, "is the stockholders' report." He held up a single sheet of paper. "I made only one copy, and after everybody has seen it, I'll destroy it." He put the single sheet on the kitchen counter and smoothed it. Deitsch, Price, and Carmody gathered loosely to look. It was on Four Talents, Ltd., letterhead stationery, and it read:

STOCKHOLDER REPORT
8 *June* '71

Gross $54,450.00
Expenses * 11,735.00
Contingency Fund   3,715.00

Net 40,000.00
Shares (4) 10,000.00

* Expenses on request. N. A.

(signed)
Sanford Campbell
President

"The television said it was sixty thousand," Sam said. Sandy did not deign to answer. "Sorry." Sam turned back to the report. There was a silence.

"What does N. A. mean?" Harry Price asked. "Not applicable?"

"No. Not audited," Sandy explained. "I couldn't very well ask Price, Waterhouse to do the books."

"Of course."

"Would you mind a hell of a lot if I asked to see the expenses, Sandy?" Carmody said. "That figure looks awful big to me."

"Not at all." Sandy produced a second sheet and lay it on the counter. It read:

EXPENSES
(*To June 8, '71.*)

Club bills and dues (arrears) $5,600.00
Club bills (current) 1,260.00
Car 300.00
Advances 2,400.00
Office equipment, telephone   1,175.00
Rental of cottage 1,000.00
Total $11,735.00

The three men who had gone into the bank became noticeably restless. They coughed, they shuffled their feet, they moved their shoulders. Somebody had to speak, and of course it was Carmody. "Sandy?" he began.

"Yes?" Sandy said brightly, open-faced, eager to answer sensible criticism.

"You're paying yourself a grand for this cottage." He looked around the pleasant little place slowly. "And eleven hundred seventy-five for this equipment and the phones. And there's almost four grand for a contingency fund. Now really, Sandy, what the hell . . ." He spread his hands, indicating, Talk to me.

"That's for the year," Sandy said helpfully.

Carmody mashed his face. "Well, it's an extra six grand for you, and tell you the truth, I didn't expect to be in this business for a whole year."

"Well, now. Well. Seen that way, it's different, of course. But very frankly I hoped we would be in business for more than a year, for many years. I was hoping I could convince all of you to reinvest."

"In what?"

"In Harry's lawsuit. In Sam's new fall line. In television commercial production, with you in charge. In real estate around here."

"Oh." Carmody looked at his palms, then at Price and Deitsch. "It's probably not a bad idea. But it's not for me." He had a cherished fantasy, and there was enough money coming to him now to realize some of it.

"That's one vote, and it can be changed, I think," Sandy said. "How about you, Harry? If we finance that survey and lawsuit of yours . . . ?"

"Well, just a minute, Sandy." Price looked curiously sightless as he spoke, a phenomenon common to actors under stress. "I'm suing for half a million bucks. If you think I'm going to take twenty grand from this outfit and feed back in five hundred thousand, you're crazy."

"Of course I don't expect that. We can work it out," Sandy said reasonably. "What about you, Sam?"

"Me?" Sam looked astonished he was asked. "No! Absolutely not! Pay me and I'll go home. I don't care about expenses, contingencies. I'm out."

"Really? Why?"

"My mother God rest her soul kept me straight on the Lower East Side—Yes, the Lower East Side, like in the movies—she said, Start out stealing from pushcarts, you end up stealing from pushcarts.' This outfit, you could make a million dollars and one day there's not going to be enough to go around and somebody, maybe you, maybe Jack, will say 'I know a little bank,' and we'll all be off again, and tell you the God's truth, gentlemen, it ain't worth it. I'm sorry I went once and I'll never go again. I'll take my money now and may God bless every one of you."

"Well!" Sandy said. "I guess that settles that." He went to the table and picked up three sealed envelopes full of money. "It's your decision, gentlemen. I think you're wrong, of course, but that doesn't matter. Here are your shares. I will split up the balance, the contingency fund, and the rentals, and will deliver the balance to you. Count your money before you—" The telephone rang.

The telephone rang and a button lit up. The men looked at one another in consternation but without alarm. "That's our first call," Sandy said. "That's the first time that telephone has rung since I had it installed."

"Answer it," somebody said.

The phone rang again, and again. Sandy put his hand on the instrument as if to stop the ringing. It rang again. He lifted the receiver. "Hello," he said. "Hello, Mister Hayden. Of course I remember you. From the bank. Yes. How did you get this number?" Oh, bright of voice. Cheerful.

"Ah, yes. My daughter. Oh, NoNoNoNo. She. She. She. Was right to give you the number. I only asked because I just had the phone installed and I didn't . . ." Sandy laughed.

"Well, of course you can. Certainly. Can you give me some idea what it's about?

"Me, too. Neither do I. I don't like the telephone, either. Why don't you come by . . . about six?

"Well, I, ah, no. There won't be anybody . . . What do you mean anybody here? My children . . .

"I see. NoNoNoNo. I'm not having guests. Why don't I plan to see you about six? You know where it is? Ha, ha, ha.

"Good. Six then. Good-bye."

Sandy hung up. He looked at his comrades, grey-green to a man, and said, "That was Hayden. He's manager of the Vista bank. He wants to see me. Tonight at six."

"What does he want?" asked a man who shall be nameless.

"He didn't say," Sandy said evenly. "But we may have a partner. Sorry, gentlemen, but put your envelopes back on the table."

13

Absalom Returns

EVERYBODY HAD AN IDEA of what to do with Hayden. Carmody, of course, wanted to put him in the hot Pontiac and roll it off a cliff. But cooler thinking indicated that if Hayden wanted them arrested, he would have called the police, not Sanford Campbell, and therefore what he probably wanted was a split, a share, and they would all have to tighten their belts a notch or two. By coming to them, Hayden became as guilty as any of them, and Sandy was cautioned not to be extravagant in his offers. Sam voiced a strong hunch that Hayden wanted to speak to Sandy on an entirely different matter, but it was only a hunch, so he didn't build a case on it. Nobody could offer a clue as to how they had been identified.

It was left to Sandy to negotiate alone. Carmody, naturally, wanted to force an outcome, and only with unanimous urging was he persuaded to go home and wait. Sandy told Brady and the kids he had an important visitor coming on confidential business, and he would be using the living room, and on no account was he to be interrupted. That established, hopefully—the children had short memories and his orders carried little dread—Sandy went out front to greet Hayden on arrival. He discovered some shrubs he had planted long ago and forgotten, and was promising them attention, when a car pulled into the driveway.

It was a recent Plymouth, green and newly washed. Out of it, also apparently newly washed, stepped Malcolm Hayden, dressed for serious business.

"Good evening, Mister Hayden. Glad you could make it."

"Mal Hayden, Mister Campbell," Hayden said, offering his hand.

Sandy took the hand without enthusiasm. "Mal. Call me Sandy. Come on inside." They entered through a front door that was rarely used, into a foyer that was largely ornamental, and passed to the living room. "Please sit down," Sandy said. "Would you like a drink?"

"I think not until I've said my piece." Hayden sat and smiled.

Be careful what your piece is. You might be found in a hot Pontiac at the bottom of a cliff. "All right. I'll have a drink when you do," Sandy said. "What's on your mind?" He sat, and tried to relax everything but his mind.

"I asked that this meeting be private because I find myself caught between what I think is right and what, for several reasons, I think I must do . . ."

"Yes." *If he knew Carmody he would think long thoughts about what he must do.*

"And what I think I must do is not what I consider right at all." He looked up sadly-brightly.

"Go on." *Is he trying to set me up for half?*

"We are new to this community and don't know anybody, and my wife is alone all day, and she—we, I guess—would like to join the Southport Country Club. I personally don't think we're ready for that kind—"

"Join the Club?" Sandy cried in disbelief. "Join the Southport Club!"

Hayden could not meet Sandy's eyes. "I was afraid you'd feel that way. I told my wife we weren't ready for that kind of thing, new to the town and me not that far up the ladder yet. (*He wants to get into the Club? Is this a rib?*) But she insisted. She can be very insistent." Hayden looked up. "She was an only child." He spread his hands as though that explained just about everything.

"I see." Sandy discovered he could not look at the man any longer, at his oiled and thinning pompadour, without bursting into laughter. He went to the cocktail wagon. "Drink?" he said.

"Well, I guess I've said my piece. Yes, I'd like a drink." Hayden sounded thoroughly discouraged.

"Oh, don't give up," Sandy said. He had two large scotches in hand and gave one to Hayden. "I think I can help you. I *know* I can, in fact. I have friends on the Membership Committee. If you're sure it's what you want."

"Oh, I'm sure it's what I want, all right," Hayden said. He could not wait to get home, and take off all his clothes, and tell his wife the good news.

"Well, I'll set the thing in motion, and get a couple of people to stand up for you. There'll be some forms to fill out, and a formal application. I'll drop by the bank with them." Relieved of a horrid burden of beastly anxiety, Sandy was inclined to largesse.

"It's really very nice of you to do this for me."

Sandy smiled at his own generosity. "It's really not all that much trouble. You're with a bank, you're presentable . . . Which reminds me, I saw you on television the other night. Thursday? Friday?"

"Friday. We had a hold-up."

"That must have been frightening."

"I was afraid," Hayden said sensibly. "I did what they told me."

"Were you able . . ." *Careful now.* "Could you identify any of the men?"

"Oh, no. But it doesn't matter. They never get picked up that way, anyway. Everybody gives a different description."

"I see," Sandy said. "Well. How do they get picked up?" He kept an incurious smile resolutely pasted to the front of his face.

"The money is baited, and it starts showing up in one area and the police and the FBI and the insurance people go into the area and pretty soon they make arrests." Hayden sipped his drink as though he did not much like scotch, then bravely sipped again to show manners.

"Baited?" Sandy coughed. "How baited?"

"I don't think it would be a breach of security to tell *you*." Hayden laughed shortly. "When the money comes in, we take serial numbers at random and record them. All denominations. The bonding companies insist on it. Sooner or later the baited money starts showing up in one area. White Plains, maybe, or a neighborhood in Brooklyn, and the police go in and talk to merchants and bankers and informers, find out who has a lot of money all of a sudden. Then they make arrests." Hayden spread his hands again, this time to show how easy it all was.

"Oh, then all that money . . ." Sandy found himself gesturing toward his cottage, and lowered his thumb quickly. ". . . can't simply be spent, can't even be deposited in a bank, or it will be traced to the area . . . in which of course it is spent or deposited." *You are talking too much.*

"Unless they're syndicate or mafia. Then they have ways of cleaning the money through race tracks or Las Vegas or loan-sharking or investing in legitimate business."

"I see," Sandy said, as though dismissing the baiting of money. "Well, it must have been quite a shock to you and a pretty terrible loss for the bank."

"Oh, I don't know." Hayden smiled. "I lived through it. The bank is insured. And the robbery might just have put the Vista Plaza on the map. We were dying there, you know. Yesterday was by twice the biggest day the A & P ever had, and Chessy's, the discount store, was jammed."

"It's an ill wind," Sandy began, and started laughing in a way that reminded Hayden old blood lines run to insanity. "Never mind," he said, recovering in part. "Have another drink." They talked through a second drink of the Club, and membership, and Hayden left with every assurance of acceptance. He drove swiftly home, beginning already to ache, to tell Jean the news and to be, please God, rewarded.

Sandy went directly out back to the cottage and called his partners and told them Hayden wanted to join their Club and that he was putting him up and they were seconding him. He set up an all hands meeting for Monday afternoon, and arranged to have breakfast with Carmody. Then he plugged in his electric typewriter and wrote plans for the cleaning of the money until well into the morning.

They sat beneath Carmody's green-and-white canopy, drinking coffee and eating hot fresh doughnuts Sandy had brought from town. When Sandy talked about Hayden's membership in the Club, Carmody got up and paced. When he started explaining the baiting and cleaning of money, Carmody became so impatient he literally climbed a tree. He straddled a beech limb, tightening his canopy with angry knots. "What you're telling me," he said when Sandy had finished, "is that I gotta get this swine into the Club when you know I got myself on the Membership Committee to stem the flow of bland WASP bankers, to keep out lumps like Hayden." He hung from the limb and dropped to the ground, not lightly but strongly.

"You'll survive this once," Sandy said, a little weary of dramatics.

"Oh, sure. I'll live through it. But what you're also telling me is I can't have my money until it's been invested in Harry's lawsuits and Sam's pants suits, which is what you wanted in the first place."

"Do you see any choice?"

"No. What I see is if you get me to agree, when there's nothing in it for me, Harry and Sam will gladly go along because there's money and work in it for them."

"I wouldn't say there's nothing in it for you," Sandy said. "You can draw a grand a month, and the company will still pick up your bar tab. That's a long way from nothing."

"Yeah." Carmody sat and sniffed at his cold coffee. "It's more than fair. Except it's not what I came for, and when I don't get what I came for I become disorderly and unmanageable. But I'll go along with you, and I'm sure the others will, too."

"Fine," Sandy said. "Now tell me what it was you came for."

"Oh, that . . ." Carmody laughed shyly. "In my second adolescence, or my dotage, I'm not sure which it is, I wanted to make a new beginning. My marital situation is worse than gentlemen are supposed to discuss. And I wanted a lump sum in hand to hold me while I got an apartment in the City and a small job somewhere. . . . To have lunch with friends once in a while, and drinks with friends at night . . ." He did not mention women.

"Well now, you know, that's not impossible. We need some kind of headquarters in the City." It pieced together so well, Sandy got excited. "Why not an apartment? You could work out of it, you and Harry, selling commercials, and you could live in it five nights and come out weekends. Why not?"

"I give up," Carmody said. "Why not?" He was getting pretty much what he came for, and was agreeable again.

"This way there won't be any separation or divorce and splitting up property," Sandy said, carried on by his enthusiasm. "You can get along with Helen two days a week, for heaven's sake, or you're crazy. Why don't we do that?"

"You're my leader," Carmody said. "You know, you're pretty smart for a member of the ruling class."

Sandy came down from his minor high. What an impossible man to deal with. "Thanks," he said.

Wednesday morning Harry Price flew to Los Angeles with twenty thousand dollars cash in his briefcase, and deposited the money to his account at the Beverly Hills branch of the Bank of America. He had lunch with Bob O'Brien of Immelman & Kurnitz, an accounting firm specializing in motion picture distribution, and authorized a box-office survey of *Hargate's Daughters*, a film Harry had produced and directed for twelve-and-one-half percent of the gross net receipts, and for which he had been paid not a dime. He gave O'Brien a check for five thousand dollars as down payment, and urged him to get cracking. At six, Harry had drinks with Jerry Roth of Hallowell, Shaw, Embry & Carstairs, eminent showbiz lawyers, and gave Roth a retainer of three thousand to institute proceedings against Sid Kransky d/b/a Allied Universal Productions, as soon as the survey results were available. He remained in California one extra day to sign appropriate papers at the accounting and law offices, and flew home Thursday night. At this peculiar juncture of personal and career matters, he thought it best not to absent himself from his wife for undue lengths of time. If this demonstrated a lack of faith in his wife and his partners, then it demonstrated a lack of faith in his wife and his partners.

Sam Deitsch took fifteen hundred dollars of baited cash to each of three Seventh Avenue factors and paid interest in advance on three ninety-day ten-thousand-dollar notes, commencing on demand. It was a practice called "hiring money" and was common on the fringe of the garment industry. That gave the Talents access to thirty thousand dollars on demand, and would provide an outlet for baited money in the future. Factors never, absolutely never, recorded serial numbers, because they were often used by the syndicate to clean money.

Sandy was in his element, playing the only game he knew, business, and playing it with relish. He dispatched Harry to the Coast and Sam to Seventh Avenue with large sums, and he deposited Harry's (Betsy's) money in the Four Talents account and drew checks on it for advances and expenses. He still had thirty thousand dollars of baited money under a mattress, yet to be cleaned, but he was in no hurry, and knew that if he did not hurry, he could clean it all safely.

It remained for Carmody to mop up. Tuesday night, Guard night, he returned the carbines to the Battalion Armory, and took the chit he had signed from the files and put it in his pocket. All day Wednesday, Carmody buffed and polished the hot Pontiac, although he did not really fear fingerprints, and Thursday morning he drove the car to the Greenwich station and left it in the lot. He put in a nervous few minutes on the platform, waiting for the train, but once aboard he sighed and settled back. He opened his *Times* to "Apartments To Let, Furnished," and began looking for a nice roomy apartment in midtown.

He also cleaned things up for Mal Hayden. Carmody was on the Membership Committee, which was leverage, and the application for membership was signed by Sanford Campbell, and endorsed by Carmody, Harry Price, and Samuel B. Deitsch, all estimable citizens. Because it was judged important by the partners to keep Hayden happy—or at least neutralized, out of everybody's hair—Carmody also arranged for a small cocktail party in the Haig Room to introduce Hayden and his wife to the others on the Membership Committee and their wives. It was an uncommon practice, reserved for very special prospective members, and virtually guaranteed acceptance.

Whenever, except in sleep, Sam Deitsch saw himself entering the Vista bank, he pushed the image out, concentrating on his wristwatch, or on exactly what somebody was saying and why, or on plans for the revival of his business. At first the image was clear and frequent and deeply disturbing, but after only days of pushing at it, it lost clarity and frequency, and became depersonalized. The robbery became something he knew well, had seen first hand, but had not taken part in. Only in dreams did the vision persist, and even in dreams his mind came to alter the circumstances, entering him into crowded rooms and airline terminals, so he could get some sleep. He discovered that Carmody had been right. If you pushed something out of your mind hard enough, it went.

On Friday morning, indulging his new luxury of sleeping late, Sam was disturbed by raucous exhaust sounds, and was more awake than asleep when Joanna entered the bedroom. He reached for her hand to pull her into bed with him. Joanna caught his hand and held it hard. "Sam," she said. "Jerry's here." Sam sat up straight, wide awake, in his mind a vision immediate as his thumb: he was walking into the Vista bank with a gun. "Tell him I'll be right down." He got up and reached for clothes.

"There's somebody with him. A big kid," Joanna said, with just the beginning of fright.

"Go ahead down," Sam said, dressing. "Don't worry about it," he added, whatever that meant. He put on old clothes, his leisure attire, and went down the back stairs to the kitchen. There were two bearded motorcycle toughs sitting at his kitchen table, one with an earring, the other his son. Joanna in a robe hugged herself by the sink. Long ago she would have showered Jerry with questions about his welfare, but that was long ago. "Hello, Jerry," Sam said. "Joanna, go someplace. Upstairs, downstairs, outside. Please." Very slowly Joanna removed herself toward the downstairs door. "What brings you here?" Sam said to Jerry.

"Business," Jerry said.

"Business with me?" Sam saw that Joanna had closed the downstairs door behind her. "I don't think so. Introduce me to your friend."

Jerry stared at him coldly for a count of ten, then inclined his head. "This is Peetah. Peetah, Sam. Peetah is our big fella." Jerry smiled. Peetah's blunt, bearded face registered nothing at all.

"What do you and Peetah want?" Sam wished Carmody were beside him.

"Money. Money from you."

"I don't have any money now. You know that." Did he know about Vista?

Jerry snorted politely. "You own a house. A big house. Free and clear. I know that much."

It was not Vista but something else. "You got your last cent from me, Jerry."

"I don't think so. I think you bought a stolen car. A 1965 Pontiac convertible, white—"

"No, I didn't," Sam said firmly. They knew nothing about the bank. They were blackmailing him for the car. Fine.

"—registered to one Arthur Jamison of the Bronx, last seen at Yankee Stadium, delivered to you at three in the afternoon, June 4th, at the Greenwich station. Paid for by you and picked up there—"

"Not by me. I don't know anything about it." It was good Carmody was not beside him, or there would be violence and bodies to no purpose.

"Don't get wise, Sam." Jerry got up and Peetah got up with him. Peetah was not so tall as he appeared sitting down, but he was big enough, thick through. "Use your head and start talking money now," Jerry said. "I don't have to go to the cops. All it takes is an anonymous tip. . . ."

"I don't know any thing about a stolen car." Sam smiled. To be threatened with car theft! Him, Eight, who had knocked over a bank! "If you're going to call the police, you better hurry, because I'm calling them right now. This is a shakedown."

Sam started for the wall phone and Peetah stepped in front of him, something gleaming on his hand. Without pause or thought Sam smashed him in the face. It was a blow of inhuman velocity and strength, fueled by years of Absalom despair and months of poverty and worry and recent weeks of awful anxiety. The blow took Peetah utterly by surprise, and he collapsed to the floor, back against the wall, blood gushing with each heartbeat from his crumpled nose. On one hand covering his face was a metal bar. There was blood on his earring. Jerry backed along the sinkboard toward the dining room, calling "Peetah! Pete! Get up! Get up, for Chrissakes!" Sam continued on to the wall phone and dialed the operator. When she came on the line, he said, "Operator, get me the police."

That brought Joanna out from behind the downstairs door, all hair and eyes. She carried an old portable radio by its strap, the only weapon available at the head of the stairs. She ran right at Sam, who covered his head, and shut the phone off with her free hand. "Hang up!" she ordered. Sam hung up. "Jerry, get in here!" Jerry came to the middle of the kitchen, watching the radio always. "You've got something on your father and now he's got something on you. You're even. All you get from the police is jail for both of you. Stolen cars! Blackmail! Extortion! What kind of family did I raise?

"You listen to me, Jerry. You pick up your stupid thug friend and get out of my house and stay out. You're not *my* son, and next time I won't have a radio in my hand, I'll have a gun! There'll be jail for me, not you! Now pick up beat-em-up Charlie and get out!"

Jerry went carefully around Sam to Peetah, and helped Peetah to his feet and out the back door. "Come back you go to *jail!*" Joanna shrieked after them. There was a silence, then the sounds of motorcycles, and they were gone.

"Now you," Joanna said to Sam. "You had that car. White Pontiac convertible. Brady told me about it." She sat at the kitchen table, where Jerry had been sitting. "You have something on your mind you should have told me weeks ago, and I want you to tell it to me now." She put the radio on the table between them.

Sam sat where Peetah had been sitting, drained of anger and strength. He paused only to decide where to begin, then took a deep breath and began with the lunch with Sandy Campbell, and told his wife the entire story of the robbery of the Vista bank. When Joanna delivered judgment on him and his crime, he realized he should have taken her into his confidence long ago, should have told her everything right from the beginning. Joanna said, "Next time steal your own car. It's easy enough. *Kids* do it."

14

The Vista Bank
Veterans Association Frolic

As a broker, then a securities analyst, and most recently an officer of a mutual fund, it was Sandy Campbell's business to understand other people's businesses and profit from them. When a business was new, or an old firm had a new idea, Sandy had one phrase he listened for: "These things take time." Whereupon he suspended investment and let somebody else pay for development time. Now he heard "these things take time" all about him, even heard himself say it. To the extent that, in another capacity, he would not have invested in Four Talents but would have waited until the "time" had elapsed, and the venture was about to flourish, then he would have bought in.

But Sam's business took time, and money, and there would be no return until first deliveries were made in November. Carmody had contracts for commercials, but they were cost-plus-residuals contracts and there would be no big money from Carmody until fall. Price's lawsuits might take a year or more to collect on. Sandy planned to build on the property behind his house, and building was a way to make good money, but it took time. By a simple projection, at the current rate of expenses, Four Talents would be looking around for financing by mid-October.

Sandy remembered having a lunch, in his early days on Wall Street, with a spare, dry, eccentric old man who turned purple explaining his need for financing. "These things take *time!*" he had howled. "Goddam *time!*" The old nut had owned all patents on the first practical disposable diaper. Nobody had invested.

Carmody pushed open the door and almost helped Harry Price into the apartment. "Sit down. Rest a minute," he said. "Let me get you a drink."

Harry collapsed in a sling chair. "Where did all the furniture go?" he said.

"I stored it in the basement. There was too much to fall over." He handed Price a drink and sat on a couch. "You're too much, Harry. I've seen directors who got things done, but you're absolutely the best."

"At those prices we gave them plenty of time," Harry said. "Put in a couple of extra studio days if you want, we'll show a profit. I'll edit tomorrow and have five, six prints for you the first of the week."

"Terrific," Carmody said. "I've got a hundred people waiting to see them." He lifted his glass and toasted. "Here's to crime," he said, and drank.

Price drank. Neither spoke for a time. Then Price said, "I hope this joint isn't bugged. . . . Of course not. Anyway, before we went into that bank I couldn't believe I was going in, and now that we've been in and out again, I can't believe I was ever there." He laughed in a kind of apology. "You feel that way?"

Carmody got up and put more scotch in his scotch and water. "No," he said. "I knew I was going in and I knew I was coming out, and I also knew I would forget it, and I almost have."

"That's a nice trick. Congratulations."

"Thank you."

"I sort of wonder about Deitsch and Sandy," Harry said. "What they tell themselves. Especially Sam, he's so vulnerable." He was thinking of the Sam who had a crush on Betsy.

"Ah. Sam's the easy one. He's learning to forget it. He told me so. Then one day something will happen and he'll tell his wife all about it—"

"Really?"

"Trust me. And when Joanna knows, Sam won't be troubled any more."

"You said he's the easy one," Price said.

"Yes. Sandy's got trouble. Old Yankee family, St. George's, Dartmouth, WASP-Wall Street, upright, uptight . . . Wow. He, stole, money. He will never forget it or forgive himself."

"They all steal money," Harry said angrily. "From farmers and widows. That's what Wall Street is all about."

"But they clean it up with a lot of rituals, like bankers. There's no ritual cleans up a holdup." Carmody sighed heavily. "That was why I was glad he had to be wheelman. If he went in with us he would have said or done something to give himself away and get punished. As it was, he tried to get us pinched for speeding, getting away."

"Poor Sandy," Price said. "Nice wife, though."

"A beauty. And just as crazy as the law allows." Carmody laughed. Not agreeing, Price said nothing. "You sure you won't stay in town for dinner?" Carmody asked.

"No, thanks. I have to get home to Betsy and Sam."

"Sam?"

"Yeah. He's got a crush on Betsy. Shows up at the damnedest times. 'To have a drink,' he says. Christ, he hates drinking." Harry made a small backhand gesture of dismissal. "Besides, I don't see much future in two men having dinner alone."

"Oh," Carmody said. "I didn't mean necessarily alone."

At five-oh-five on Friday, bursting with good news and vital juices, Mal Hayden careened homeward from the bank in his recent Plymouth. Sandy Campbell had come in to cash his unemployment check—five days late, apparently he was in no great money squeeze—and to invite the Haydens to cocktails next Wednesday at the Southport Country Club. "Not a big affair," Campbell had said. "Meet a few of the members who are putting you up. And their wives. Meet some of the Membership Committee, their wives. Dress pretty much as you're dressed now. Stop by my house about five. Small drinks. We'll go over." Campbell had spoken in stilted, staccato sentences, and seemed foolishly nervous in the bank, and eager to be someplace else. "And for heaven's sake don't mention my unemployment. To any one."

"Hoo-hoo-hoo Mamma!" Hayden howled, racing breakneck on a narrow road. "Poppa's comin' home." He had not called his wife from the bank with the news so she would not have time to grow a headache, or gas, before he got home. "Hoo-eee Mamma!" he howled again, narrowly missing a cement truck. "Here I come!" Hayden was thirty-two, prized by his employers for his prudence and industry, and where his wife was not concerned, not a fool at all.

Mal did not especially notice Westport when he crossed that gilded town line, nor did he feel any pride in his fine new neighborhood, and although he had put together forty-six thousand dollars for the house, he could not properly say that it was colonial, ranch, Tudor, or split. He had acquired all these things for his wife, and not as gifts of love but as bribes for access to her person. He stopped his car in the driveway and gathered up a bottle he had bought for Jean. Whisky sometimes moved her. It seemed he could not get enough air into his chest, walking toward the house. He tingled with anticipation from his nipples to his knees, going through the door. He put the bottle on a counter and called "Hello!" cheerfully, trying to sound relaxed and normal, in the sense sane.

"I'm upstairs," Jean called.

"I'll be right up!"

"No! No! I'll come down!" They both raced for the stairs and met in the middle. "Hi," Jean said, and bent to be kissed.

Mal put his arms around her thighs and buried his face in her belly, swooning in softness and fragrance. He felt Jean stiffen after a time and let go. "Good news!" he cried. "Come on. Let's have a drink." He turned and led the way down the stairs to the kitchen.

"I don't think there is anything."

"I got a bottle of Seven on the way home." Mal got out two tall glasses and 7-Up and crashed and smashed ice cubes loose from a rarely used ice tray.

"What's the good news?" *Oh-oh. Good news on Friday night. I'm supposed to be happy until Monday morning.*

"Not until we have a drink." Mal measured Seven Crown in a shot glass and poured it over the ice, then added 7-Up to the brim of both glasses. He handed a drink to Jean and lifted his own in toast. "Here's to Southport Country Club," he said, and drank.

"Really? What happened?"

"Take a sip first." Jean did. "*We* have been invited to *cock*-tails to meet some *mem*-bers on *Wen*-sdy."

Well thank God I sort of feel like it anyway. "Wednesday!" Jean cried. "What'll I wear?"

"Campbell said nothing special. He said dress like I was." Mal held out his arms to show how he was dressed, and Jean ran into his arms and kissed him and bubbled at how wonderful things were. They left their drinks scarcely touched in the kitchen in order not to spill them on the wall-to-wall upstairs.

Jean dozed now. Mal drew a finger along her spine to the hollow at her waist and into the auburn down below and smoothed one gracious buttock many times with his palm and eased his hand into her warmth. "Nnnnh," Jean said, waking in part. "Let's take a shower," Mal said, massaging her. "You'll feel like it again after a shower." "I took a shower before you got home," Jean said. "Take another one, with me." "Nnnnh." "Come on," Mal pleaded. "Nice and clean," he added witlessly, nodding hard. "All right," Jean said. "But then dinner, okay?" "Okay," Mal said (anything).

Brady Campbell had just trounced Joanna Deitsch at golf, and collected some change from her, and felt perfectly splendid. She drove Joanna home, and pulling into the Deitsches' driveway remarked a small foreign car parked before the house. "Who's that?" she asked.

"It's Helen Carmody's car," Joanna said. "I wonder what she wants."

"Well, let's see." Brady shut off her car. She had not meant to stay, but perhaps Carmody had beaten Helen and she had come to the Deitsches for sanctuary.

There was no one in the kitchen or anywhere on the first floor. Joanna put her head in the downstairs doorway and called "Hello?"

"In the bedroom!" Sam called from upstairs.

Joanna turned to Brady. "What is she doing in the bedroom?"

Brady, who thought of sex only when she was in bed, shrugged. "Talking to Sam, I guess," she said.

"Well. Would you like a Coke or something? How about some lunch?" Joanna plugged in the coffeepot and opened the refrigerator door and closed it and let some water run in the sink. "Where are my girls?" she demanded. "Where *is* everybody?"

"They're at my house," Brady said firmly. "Now relax." She was firm because she thought Joanna was being a poor sport about losing a little at golf. She could see nothing else amiss.

Joanna went to the back stairs. "Are you coming down?" she yelled.

"When we're finished!" Sam answered.

"I see," Joanna said furiously. "I see." She went to the refrigerator and emptied it on the kitchen table, prepared to force-feed Brady lunch to keep her around. "Some wonderful cold cuts," she pleaded. "Rye bread Sam brings up from the City. Kosher spears, homemade mustard. Have a sandwich." There was a timid knock on the back screen door. "Now who can that be?" Joanna asked the air, and went to the back hall.

It was Betsy Price. "Hello," Betsy said. "May I come in?"

"Well. Well. Look who's here! Come in!" What? Was Samuel B. Deitsch now a sex symbol? "Brady, you know Betsy." The two women said Hello. "Well. What brings you by, although God knows you're welcome . . . ?"

"Oh, Sam has been dropping off at our place to say hello, so I thought I'd make a call on you." Joanna seemed still bewildered. "It's protocol," Betsy added.

"Well. Fine. You're just in time for some lunch."

"Thanks," Betsy said, sitting at the table, "but I just finished breakfast."

"Maybe a . . . drink, then?"

"Oh, no. It's much too early. Where are all the beautiful daughters Sam talks about?" To Brady: "I've never heard a man talk so lovingly of his family. Everything is Joanna and Susan and Toni and Lisa . . ."

"Lori," Brady said. "Not Toni. They're at my house for the day."

"Two out of three's not bad," Betsy said, a little sharply. She did not much enjoy the company of women. "I'd like some ginger ale if you have it, Joanna. It's thirsty out."

"That sounds good," Brady said. "I'll have some too." Footsteps were heard on the back stairs.

"Take Cokes," Joanna said distractedly, banging cans on the table. She watched the back stairs doorway as though hunted from there. Sam appeared, beaming and calling Good Morning. Behind him on the stairs was Jack Carmody. "You!" Joanna said. Carmody recoiled at her anger. "No. Ethel Merman," he said. "What are you doing with your wife's car?" "Ah," Carmody said, and smiled, "I see." He laughed lightly, which made Joanna madder. "Have some lunch," she ordered. "Or I suppose you'd rather have a drink." "Well now. What time is it?" Carmody's eyes found the stove clock. "Eleven-thirty. Time for a drink, I would say. Betsy will join me, won't you, Bets. And Brady . . . ?" "It's after one!" Joanna cried. "The stove clock's been broken for five *years!*" And she heard herself, and she started to laugh, hard. At Carmody, of course, but mostly at herself, for her folly. Her laughter filled the astonished room with heart, and forced a mood.

"I might have a drink," Brady said. "Just a small one. Might give me an appetite." "I will if you will," Betsy said, stating her case honestly.

"Help me get some booze, Jack," Sam said. "It's downstairs." "Buried?" They went down the stairs and to a closet with seemingly hundreds of bottles on shelves and unopened case goods on the floor. "Mercy!" Carmody said reverently. "Look at all that booze!" "Grab some bottles. Take what you like," Sam said. They each took several dusty bottles. "I got a price in the City," Sam explained, climbing the stairs. "From my cousin. So I bought a dozen cases. A lifetime supply for me." "You *will* need help drinking it all," Carmody said, by inference volunteering. In the kitchen, he took charge. "Just ice and glasses please, Joanna. Betsy will have a martini-rocks, I know, and perhaps we can persuade Brady to join her." "Just a small one," Brady said. "Just a little of the white meat," Carmody mocked politely. "*I* will have a scotch on the rocks. What's for you, Sam?" "I just got up." "Fine. Two scotch-rocks," Carmody decided. "Joanna?" "Nothing for me." "I respect your wishes."

"May I use the telephone?" Brady asked. "Of course," Sam said. "Help yourself." Brady went to the wall phone and dialed. "I'll have a little vermouth, after all," Joanna decided. "Excellent stomachic," Carmody agreed. He placed a drink in Betsy's hand. "Stir it with your finger." He put a martini at Brady's place at the table, which he stirred with his finger, then sucked the finger. "Ambrosia," he said, "but murder. Not for us career chaps." Brady said from the phone, "My husband's hungry, wants me to feed him." To Betsy she said, "Harry's over there." "I know," Betsy said. "Tell them come on over," Carmody said. "Tell them pick up Helen and come on over," Joanna amended. "Must we?" Carmody asked. "Shush," Joanna said. "Scotch-rocks for you, Sam." Carmody handed Sam a drink. "And a scotch-rocks for me. First of the day," he lied, for no special reason. Brady hung up. "They'll pick up Helen and be right over," she said. "Oh, darn," said Carmody elegantly. "Shush," Joanna said again.

"Sandy and Harry got some project going?" Sam asked. He had found a comfortable perch on the kitchen counter, with a cabinet to rest his head against. "Seach me," Brady said vaguely. "Good idea," Carmody said. "Wait till the other men get here and we'll have a gang-search." "Jack!" Joanna said. She was protective of Brady's innocence. "Have you ever been gang-searched?" he asked Betsy. "No," Betsy said, "but I was once under contract to Paramount, which is roughly the same thing." She much preferred talking to men. "Excellent. Then you will instruct Brady as to the ritual of surrender," Carmody said. "Perfume her hair, anoint her person, et cetera." "Jack, stop it," Joanna said. Because Brady did not talk sex, a lot of women thought she was simple and needed protection, and Joanna was one of them.

"Dark eyes sparkling angrily," Carmody said. "Let's do *Ivanhoe.* You can be Rebecca and Betsy can be Rowena and Sandy when he gets here is a natural Ivanhoe. . . ." "I did Rowena in high school," Brady said. "You've ripened," Carmody said graciously.

"No. Let's do *Lear,*" Betsy said. "You'd make a gas of a Lear, Jack." "Why thank you," Carmody said, flattered. "Harry can be the bastard—what's his name?—Edmund. Harry can be a real bastard when he wants to. Brady can be a daughter. We can all be daughters. Sam can be the . . . ah . . . other guy, the love interest." Betsy fell silent. She had been about to cast Sam as Fool.

"Sam is Hamlet," Joanna said definitely. "I've lived with him half my life and take my word he's Hamlet." "What a nice thing to say," Brady said. Sam said, "Thank you, Joanna, thank you." He knew Betsy had meant him for Fool. "You think all that much,

Sam?" Carmody asked. "Think, worry, fret, eat his heart out," Joanna said. "That's my Sam." "It looks good on you, Sam," Carmody said. "Keep it up."

Helen Carmody came in the door followed by Sandy Campbell and Harry Price. The two men did not at first know how to react to the minor drinking bout begun without them, but Helen did. She was in her best old-buddy mood, and why not? Two attractive men, not family, had come by in a smashing Pontiac-Rolls on a fine June morning to take her to a party. She went to her husband and kissed him on the cheek, then directly to the bottles to make herself a martini. Her husband did not make martinis for her. "Hi, everybody," she said when her drink was made, "Let's have a Saturday!"

"Beautifully put," Harry said, going to the booze. "Beautifully put. I think I shall indeed have a Saturday. Fix you a drink, Sandy? Anybody?" "Put a little on top of this," Betsy said, handing him an empty glass. "I'm starved," Sandy said, looking at the food on the table. "Nobody goes hungry in my house," Joanna declared, and took food from the refrigerator like clowns coming from a car in the circus. "Have a small drink for manners first," Harry said, and handed him a scotch. Sandy took the glass and struck the posture, without at all striking a posture, of Dink Stover after tennis.

"Betsy, your husband is here and my wife is here, and now I can with propriety invite you downstairs to see something beautiful." Carmody spoke, of course. "I've already seen it," Betsy said. Brady shouted with laughter. "Don't be coarse, love. This is transcendental." Betsy got up and Carmody took her hand and led her down the stairs to the liquor closet and threw open the door. "Oh, that's beautiful!" Betsy cried. She put an arm about Carmody's waist and rested her soft hair against his shoulder. Carmody put his arm fondly around her. Together they gazed into the liquor closet. "It's all yours, Bets," he said, voice thick with emotion. "Twelve cases."

"It's ours, darling. Not mine but *ours*," Betsy said dreamily. "Two cases of Gordon's gin! Oh, Jack! You've made me the happiest girl in the world!" She put her face up to be kissed and Carmody kissed her. "When I saw it I thought of you," Carmody said. "I said to myself I must get this for Betsy at whatever cost, if I must level the forest and till the plains. . . ." They kissed again and went upstairs. Harry was alone in the kitchen. "Well!" he said. "Was it really all that beautiful?" "Breathtaking!" Betsy sighed. "Can I see it?" Harry asked Carmody. "You wouldn't appreciate it," Carmody answered truthfully. "Oh," Harry said. "Well." He started for the back door with his hands full of drinks. "Where is everybody?" Betsy asked. Harry stopped at the door. "While you were down there, in ecstasy over God knows what, Sam and Sandy decided to play croquet for their wives." "Can't wives do anything for themselves?" Betsy asked. "Not that way," Harry said. He backed out, opening the screen door with his jutted bottom. "For their *wives*. Their wives' lives in servitude." He left. "I hope Sandy wins," Carmody said. "Joanna's a marvelous cook." They went to the rank of bottles and filled their glasses and went out into the sun arm in arm.

They got Helen dressed before the Deitsch girls got home, and Brady and Harry were disentangled apparently in the nick. (The downstairs couch was very like a bed.) On vermouth only, Joanna decided she was Ma Barker and these her sons and chewed a cigar and talked of bank robberies with Sandy, who had forgotten she was not supposed to know anything about Vista. They agreed to steal their own car next time. Betsy turned cold lady and would not suffer Sam to touch her lest they "sully their enchantment."

It was of course an extraordinary afternoon—grownups are so seldom permitted to play—but it broke no new ground. Impromptu afternoon debauches happen all too rarely, but they do happen, in the best of suburbs. This gathering was uniquely abandoned and long remembered because it was the first reunion of the Vista Bank Veterans Association and its almost entirely unwitting Ladies Auxiliary. The revelry was part of war, and furious.

15

Upward Social Mobility

WHEN JACK CARMODY told Meyer, the chief steward, to have Seven Crown and 7-Up available for cocktails in the Haig Room, that worthy chilled him with a glance. "Don't sneer at me, you old snob," Carmody said. "The guest of honor drinks seven-and-seven. I can't help it." "You are endorsing him for membership," Meyer said simply, and examined his nails. "Now if you will excuse me I will see to the hors d'oeuvres." He turned and left Carmody standing alone in the Haig Room's double doors.

"Permission granted," Carmody said at the steward's back. He went to the bar table before the fireplace and made himself a drink. If there had been somebody to grumble to, he would have grumbled. He had recruited himself to the Membership Committee to exclude exactly the kind of bland, acceptable swine that Hayden represented. He had thought to bring in blacks, or at least some people who didn't speak English very well, and in his first gesture as a Committee member he was endorsing a white bank branch manager with a pompadour, and endorsing him principally because he, Carmody, with a few friends, had robbed the dolt's bank. Crime does not pay.

In a keen political move, Mal Hayden called Tom Clarke, acting president of the County Trust Company, to ask for help on Wednesday. "We've been terrifically busy down here since the late unpleasantness," he laughed. "Deposits, new accounts, great business. But I've got a thing Wednesday afternoon that I really don't think I should miss. . . ."

"Well, what kind of a thing, Mal?" Clarke asked in measured, valuable tones.

"Some friends of mine are putting me up for the Southport Country Club, and Wednesday they're having—"

"The Southport Country Club."

"Yes. And they're having a small cocktail party so my wife and I can meet some of the Membership—"

"The *South*port Country Club?"

"Yes. It means a lot to my wife. We're new in the Westport community, after all. Otherwise I wouldn't take time off with things as busy here. . . ."

"No, no. You're doing the right thing. I'll send—ah—Harrison down tomorrow. You can show him around and he can cover for you Wednesday."

"Thanks," Hayden said. "I hope you understand I wouldn't take off for any ordinary cocktail—"

"Oh, no. No. I understand. Go ahead. This could be very valuable for you career-wise. Let me know how you make out."

"I understand I'm in now."

"Let me know anyway."

"I will. Good-bye and thanks, Mr. Clarke."

"Goodbye, Mal."

Hayden hung up and smiled, just vulpine, ear to ear. Maybe he had been right in the first place, and Sandy Campbell was The Man to salvage Mal Hayden's fortunes. Not the Vista Plaza, of course—the robbery had salvaged that—but Mal Hayden's personal fortunes, his marriage and his job.

"Who is he?" Brady asked. "Where did you find him?"

"He's the manager of a little bank up the road. The financing of our little company out in the cottage might just need a little bank like that pretty soon."

"I don't see why you couldn't have picked somebody from Chase or Bankers' Trust or something."

"Oh, don't be such a snob," Sandy said. "Maybe his wife will be nice. One way or another, you only have to put up with them for one afternoon."

"Well, if I don't like her, I'm not going to take her under my wing and show her around and introduce her to everybody."

"Okay," Sandy said, because the more nearly hopeless the wife was, the more Brady would help her.

Jack Carmody was paged to the telephone by muted loudspeaker. It was Helen, and she was in Stamford and her car had broken down. Jack told her to call Triple-A and he'd see her when she got there, but Helen became so wildly angry at that over the phone that he decided to drive down and pick her up then in order not to be stabbed in his sleep later. He told Meyer the steward that he would be gone the best part of an hour and asked Meyer to see that things went smoothly. He was assured with impregnable disdain that all would go perfectly well in his absence.

Just as soon as Jean Hayden spoke, Brady put her under her wing for a time. They arrived exactly at five, and Jean said she was sorry they were late but her husband was a terrible driver. "You're right on time," Brady said. "Come on in." Why did these women try to establish themselves by disparaging their husbands?

"He drives like the hammers of hell, but he has no sense of direction and gets lost all the time," Jean explained. She made a face that said "Men!"

"What a lovely dress!" Brady said, and indeed it was. "Where did you get it?" It was a simple linen sheath that belted in the middle, and unfortunately. There was something just not chic about so much figure. Perhaps she could get her to loosen the belt a trifle, before Sandy made a grab at her.

"At Saks' in White Plains," Jean said. "I get all my clothes there."

"They have nice things. Would you like a drink to carry you through this ordeal?" Brady led Jean to the booze cart.

Jean stopped, surprised. "Ordeal? My husband said the whole thing was arranged."

"I just meant meeting all those new people. (*Wow.*) I find meeting new people an ordeal sometimes," Brady said. "What would you like?"

"A seven-and-seven if you have any."

"Yes. Sandy? Do we have any seven-and-seven?"

"I'm afraid not," Sandy said. He smiled a brilliant, nervous smile at Jean because he had just seen that body. "How about a rye and ginger?"

"That would be fine," Jean said.

"And you, Mal?"

"Whatever you're drinking," Mal said, reevaluating his drinking pattern swiftly.

Brady did not know what a seven-and-seven was, but she knew who drank rye and ginger, and she would fix that as soon as she could. They had drinks, and talked small talk, chiefly about what a sublime day it was, and Sandy told the Haydens, "Just relax and enjoy yourselves. Your membership is assured unless you get drunk and swing at somebody, so just be yourselves and have a good time. Make it a party, okay?"

"Okay," Hayden said. "And in case I manage to forget somehow, I want to thank you for today." Except where his wife was concerned, he was not especially a fool.

"My pleasure," Sandy said. "Now let's get started. Shall we all go in my car or shall we take two cars?"

"I'd rather go in your car so we don't get lost," Jean said.

"No. I know where the Club is, and it's between here and home. We'll go in our car and save a trip." Mal was very politely miffed.

They went in two cars, Sandy leading. "Well, how is she?" he asked Brady.

"Nice enough, I suppose," Brady said. "I just wish she wouldn't—"

"Wouldn't throw that insane body around?" Sandy laughed.

"She does have a figure, doesn't she? No. I wish she wouldn't put her husband down every chance she gets. Reminds me of Mrs. Donovan who used to come and clean."

"Well, maybe you can cure her of that."

"Take her under my warm wing for a while," Brady suggested.

"Well, yes. Show her around a little. It's important to me right now."

"I guess so," Brady sighed.

Hayden followed so closely Sandy could only assume he was driving through a torrent of encouragement. The two cars entered the parking lot in almost one piece, and Hayden parked bumper-up to Sandy's station wagon. They got out of the cars and walked up to the terrace that faced Long Island Sound. Brady walked with Jean and Mal walked with Sandy, talking of the business boom at the Vista Plaza since the robbery put them on the map. "We always knew the people were out there somewhere. Surveys said so. It took a robbery and the television news for them to discover us."

They paused on the terrace. Off to the right the sun was lowering orange into the haze over New York City. The orange was caught in small clouds out over the Sound and on many sails. Long Island humped on the skyline, dim in the haze but there. It was a sunny evening in late June, and not hot. With the Sound glittering before her, and the faded opulence of the Club at her back, Jean Hayden felt a new beginning, like entering college or marriage, and prayed she would not be disappointed. What she hoped precisely was that she would never lose the heady sense of glamor and privilege she now felt, that the Club would never seem to her ordinary, as even her new home was becoming.

Mal Hayden took the Club much more in stride, took it, indeed, as his due. With industry and prudence and a lot of luck, you went from teller to assistant manager to manager, from Peekskill to Katonah to Westport, from nothing to something to more. The Southport Country Club was a part of the dream of life opened to him by boys' fiction, movies, *The Reader's Digest*, and, less emphatically, by television. It was becoming his because he had earned it. Campbell was The Man who got the Club for him, but according to the dream, with industry and prudence The Man would have come along, Campbell or another. If you worked hard and used your head and seized opportunities, The Man showed up. Nonetheless, he was grateful to Campbell for arranging the party for him, and the dream sustaining him, he did not then wonder why he was worth so much fuss.

There were several guests in the Haig Room when they went in. Brady and Sandy took the Haydens around the room and introduced them very informally, chatting for a few minutes with each group. They followed a haphazard kind of seniority, beginning with Mr. Lloyd Morrison, a husky, tanned old gentleman wearing, Hayden noted, blue sneakers and no socks. Mr. Morrison had learned Hayden was with County Trust and asked him many informed questions about the Vista operation, making no reference to the robbery. Because he seemed to know so much about banking, Hayden asked if he had once been a banker, to which Mr. Morrison replied, simply, "No." They continued in reverse seniority, imprecisely, meeting the Petries and the Sargents and the Fairchilds, and later meeting the younger guard—the Sinclairs and Magruders and Hansens. When Jim Sinclair heard that Mal was with County Trust, he recommended Mal get next to Mr. Morrison. "He's a trustee," Sinclair said. "Hell, he's *the* trustee." "Oh. *That* Mr. Morrison!" Hayden looked around for the old man with no socks, but he had gone. "Holy Christ," Hayden said reverently. He had been gabbing with Tom Clarke's employer, his boss's boss. He felt giddy.

The four, the Campbells and the Haydens, took a post near the front doors to greet new arrivals. After a time, Hayden voiced amazement that the Membership Committee was so large. "They're mostly freeloaders," Sandy explained, "drawn by the scent of free booze." After another time, arrivals ceased, and the four turned their attentions to the big room full of people and talk and smoke. Nobody noticed them. Hayden followed Sandy to the bar to get drinks for themselves and the girls, where Hayden lost Sandy to an urgent conversation. He had three glasses filled and went back to the door, but the women were gone. He was alone, and as guest of honor he wanted very much not to be alone, and his desire was fulfilled. A most transparently sincere man named Hamilton relieved him of one drink, asked a baseball question, and launched into an encomium on The Realtor In Modern Society. With a glass in either hand, assailed by a demonstrable nut, Mal looked around for exits like a rat in a fire. At last he saw his wife being courted—there was no other word for the angle of the man's head, the lewdness of his smile—by someone very familiar to him. He saw that it was Harry Price, whom he knew from television. "You'll have to excuse me," Mal said to Hamilton, "my wife is waving to me." Hamilton shrugged and turned away in a manner that said he had been bored and about to leave anyway.

Jean Hayden was terribly impressed at meeting *the* Harry Price, of The Harry Price Theater, although she remembered the show only dimly, from earliest childhood. "You must be *very* prematurely grey," Jean said. Their conversation had reached an intimacy where such a remark was possible. "Been this color since I was twenty," Harry said. "Just think, you're living right here in Westport," he added, and smilingly implied that distance would therefore be no obstacle to them. "And your husband is a banker.

That's wonderful!" Bankers didn't show up at home at odd hours, like used car salesmen, for example. Understanding only that she was being somehow deeply complimented, Jean smiled back hard. "Isn't your wife with you tonight?" she asked. Harry looked abruptly tragic, by inference misunderstood. "Yes, but we won't bother her now." "Oh," Jean said, seeing that he was saddened. Harry brightened with her sympathy. "You must come by some night for drinks and dinner and a late swim," he said. "I'm sure we'd love to," Jean said. "Oh, yes. Bring your husband of course." They were interrupted by the arrival of Malcolm Hayden—or at least Harry made it seem like an interruption. At first Harry could not seem to understand Hayden, then he said, "Oh, yes. Signed a paper to get you in here. Hope you enjoy it," and those devices failing to get rid of him, listened with distinct annoyance as Mal praised the Harry Price Theater and said it was what television needed more of today. "What are you doing now?" Mal asked. "Any television, I mean?"

Harry decided he would charm the peasant, then betray him, other maneuvers having failed. He smiled a famous smile. "No more television for me, old man. Had it up to here. I make motion pictures now."

"We never go to the movies any more," Jean said, citing a virtue.

"Scarcely anyone does, unfortunately," Harry said.

"Well, we go sometimes," Mal said. "Have you done anything we might have seen?"

Harry named three recent pictures.

"No. We read about them, of course, but I don't think we saw them. Were you *in* anything? I mean acting?" Hayden was curiously agitated.

"Not for years." Harry laughed a famous laugh. "Not for longer than I'd care to tell."

"It's funny . . ." Mal began.

"What's funny, old man?" Harry asked.

"Well, I don't have the feeling now, up close," Mal said, "but seeing you at a distance, across the room, the way you stood and your head moved . . . well, I had the feeling I had seen you in something recently." Hayden laughed at how silly it all was.

"Might have been re-runs," Harry offered pleasantly. "They've been re-running a lot of my old stuff. I under*stand*. I don't watch them because the actors look too young."

"Maybe that's it," Mal said weakly, because that wasn't it, but it would come to him. "Is Mrs. Price with you? Miss Cameron?"

"Let me get her for you," Harry said, breaking into a nearby group. "Betsy? Bets? Come and meet our honored guests." Betsy came toward them smiling. Perhaps she could get this clod off in a corner and amuse him while Harry Price laid seige to the clod's wife's virtue.

Later, when people were beginning to leave, Hayden found himself alone again. For something to do he went to the bar and got another drink, thinking *One at Campbell's, two here, and this makes three. Four. Nothing to worry about.* Then he saw a man come in the door whose gestures and brisk presence were disturbingly familiar. Far back in the cave of his memory there was a connection between him and this solid, blunt, rock-like, vigorous man, a connection somehow tinged with fear. It was all too bizarre and not quite sane, and Mal put his drink on a table and left it there. The blunt man went to Sandy Campbell and shook hands with him briskly, and they both looked at Hayden and started toward him. Mal smiled in tentative recognition, sure now they had met before, someplace. "Mal, this is Sam Deitsch," Sandy said. "Mal Hayden, Sam. Sam was one of your sponsors in this little affair."

Hayden shook hands. "Nice to meet you, Mr. Deitsch. Thanks very much from my wife and I."

"Nothing to it, young fella. Call me Sam. Sorry I'm late but a friend of ours . . . Sandy, listen to this. . . . Carmody went down to Stamford to pick up his wife because her car broke down and he ran out of gas on the Parkway and called me to come get his wife before he killed her." Sam laughed. "Great God, how that couple can fight!"

"Will they be along?" Sandy asked.

"Just Jack. I took Helen home." Sam laughed again. "She gave me hell all the way to Westport. You'd think it was all my fault."

"How about a drink?" Sandy said.

"Okay. Fine," Sam said.

"You, Mal?"

"I've got one, thanks," Mal said, taking up his glass from the table. Sandy left for the bar. "I don't very much need this one," he added quietly to Sam.

"I'm not much of a drinker, either," Sam confided.

"I've only had three, this makes four, and that's not much, for all evening . . ."

"No. Three or four won't hurt you."

Hayden took a long drink. "It's not the booze, anyway," he said. "It's just when you walked in the door I had the strangest feeling I knew you from someplace. Not just had *seen* you, but knew you well. That's the second time it's happened to me tonight."

"You might have seen me around town," Sam said, dismissing it. "Let's get some fresh air." He took Hayden's arm and propelled him to the French windows opening on the terrace. Sandy joined them, handed Sam a drink, and turned to contemplate the last light of a lovely summer day.

Behind Sandy, in the Haig Room, a big, big man came through the double doors and took up a challenging stance in mid-floor, looking about alertly, aggressively. Again Hayden had an imperative sense of recognition. This man he had surely seen before, and suddenly, just as surely, he knew where he had seen him. In a bank, with a ski mask on his face, with a big floppy hat on his head, with a gun in his hand. Had seen him standing just as he stood now, legs apart, challenging, roaring, "Don't muss a moovle!" Hayden backed out two small steps, onto the terrace, not to be seen.

"Here's Jack now," Sam said. He went to get Carmody. He was a brisk, solid, vigorous figure with a bouncing step. Just like the one the others had called "Eight" in the bank. Hayden's breathing became painfully shallow. The blood fell from his face, leavhis cheeks cold. The sunset colors all about him went palely bright, as at dawn. Carmody approached, Sam leading him. Sandy turned to Hayden to introduce him and saw he was down on one knee.

"What's the matter, man!"

"My God," Hayden said. "I think I'm going to faint!"

"Get your head down," Sandy said. They were on the terrace, so it was not a public performance. Sandy put his hand on Hayden's neck. "You're freezing," he said.

Mal forgot, in his fear of fainting now, here, before new friends, what he had been afraid of, and he recovered sufficiently to look up, and he saw Carmody, looking down at him from great height and with scorn, and he began fainting again. "Is he passing out?" Carmody asked.

"Not from drinking," Sandy said. "Come on. Give me a hand with him."

"Where'll we take him?"

"Not through the room. It'll embarrass everybody and embarrass him most of all. Take him down to the boathouse."

"No! I'll be all right here!" Hayden cried. "Leave me here! No!" He did not want to go anywhere with these men.

"Hush!" Sandy ordered. "Quiet!" Then more gently, "It's private there. You'll feel better in a jiffy. Grab his arm, Jack." He and Carmody hefted Hayden up between them and carried him across the terrace and down the stairs to the boathouse. In the entranceway to the boathouse were several canvas chairs. They propped Hayden up in one and loosened his tie and belt, then bent him forward again, to get blood back to his head. Sam arrived with a plump, dark woman who had smelling salts. They

called her Joanna. The salts bit cruelly at Hayden's nose and restored his senses sufficiently for him to become afraid again. He
was among thieves, desperate thieves with guns, and he was alone,
and weak and sick.

Joanna seized his forelock roughly and jammed the salts again
to his nose. More consciousness. Harry Price was one of them!
That was where he had seen Price before! Dear God, the man in
the bank had said "Splendid!" just like Harry Price on television,
and everybody had thought it was a joke. And Sandy Campbell,
his benefactor, The Man! Somebody had to be driving that get-
away car, and that somebody was Campbell, who had cased the
bank cashing his unemployment check.

The smelling salts hit him anew and he cried out in pain. And
that was why they had made such a fuss over him, a cocktail party
for the piss-ant manager of a lost branch bank! Oh, my God, he
prayed, my God. Get me out of this and I will never do anything
vain or stupid again! I will even get a divorce, or perhaps an
operation!

Carmody went back to the Club to explain to the remaining
company that the guest of honor had suffered a "touch of the
sun," but would be all right. With Carmody gone, most of the
fear was gone, and Mal came slowly back. Joanna's hand was
gentle now, and she fixed his pompadour. "There you are. You're
going to be fine," she said quietly. Harry Price arrived and stood
about looking concerned and sorry.

Sandy and Harry helped Hayden to his car, Sam and Joanna
following. Carmody was there with Jean Hayden. "He's always
doing something like this," she said crossly. Everybody offered to
drive them home, but Jean said she could manage. "Just get him
in the front seat. God!" They all helped Hayden into the car, and
Joanna bent in to fasten his seat belt around him, then they all
stood back. Hayden looked up, one last unbelieving time, at
Campbell, Carmody, Deitsch, Price, and the warm and kindly
Joanna. They all smiled, as in a photograph taken at a summer

picnic. "Hang in there, old man!" Price said encouragingly. The car started off. Everybody waved gaily. "Goodbye!" they called, and "Good luck!" "Don't worry about a thing!" Sandy shouted, last of all.

And Hayden realized that his banker's instinct had been right after all, and that Sandy Campbell was truly The Man, the savior of the Vista Plaza, and of Mal Hayden.

"Thanks a lot, Mal," Jean began. "It's like you. It's the story of our goddamned marriage. We get a chance to meet some people who *are* somebody, who *do* things, people with a little money and education. *Class* people! And you decide I'm having too good a time and you pull a faint! Why didn't you throw up while you were at it? That would have been a nice touch. Stick your finger down your throat next time." Jean went on.

Mal shut her out. He had to think about what to do with what he knew. If he called the police, he might get a medal, but he'd be out of a job soon. Tom Clarke was waiting to hear about the Southport Country Club, not about rich bank robbers. Mr. Lloyd Morrison would definitely not be gratified to learn Hayden had sent Mr. Morrison's friends to jail. If he blew the whistle he would be without access to his wife's person in perpetuity. He had, tritely enough, nothing to gain and everything to lose by calling the police.

Hayden became abruptly aware of the comic utter aloneness of his situation. Not even the bank robbers knew that he knew they had robbed a bank. He laughed sharply, interrupting his wife's tirade.

"Something's funny!" she demanded.

"No. It's nothing." And Hayden realized that if he said nothing now, to his wife, he could never say anything at all to anybody. "We're in," he said, interrupting Jean again. "You wanted the Club and I got it for you. Now shut up and drive and let's get home and go to bed."

16

The Quarterly Report

$54,450 IS AN INCONSIDERABLE sum until it disappears. If $54,450 is spent to defoliate an Indochinese shrub, why that's how much it costs, is all. If the money is known to have gone someplace—to a congressman's mistress, or a celebrity's automobile, or a Mafia treasury—then it is known to have gone someplace, and can be dismissed from mind. But when $54,450 disappears, it tears a hole in the fabric of society, and many angry forces are set in motion.

Spearheading Establishment efforts to discover where the $54,450 had gone (not to recover it; the amount was negligible) were Senior Agent George Schweitzer of the Stamford office of the Federal Bureau of Investigation, and (Papa) Carmine Pasarelli, capo of the Yonkers family that bore his name. Agent Schweitzer had at his disposal the resources of the Treasury Department—including Internal Revenue, Customs, and narcotics—of the Justice Department, Interpol, bonding and insurance company detectives, the state police of New York and Connecticut, all right-thinking citizens, and a bank of computers in Chevy Chase, Maryland. If a reasonable suspect could be discovered, Agent Schweitzer could build a case against him with electronic speed. Carmine Pasarelli had informers everywhere, and the insane smarts, and no need to build a case for no court. He and Schweitzer could make a very formidable team to elude if they had any idea, any at all, where to start looking.

Neither made any progress, but neither was dismayed. Time was their ally if they had the patience to employ it. The Vista robbery had been such a very soft touch that with all the restraint in the world the same men would rob again, and nearby. The trick was to figure out roughly where and when, and to be roughly there when they struck again.

The computer agreed. Schweitzer's men fed in everything that could be learned and programmed about the Vista robbery and dozens of similar robberies across the nation. The entire geographic, economic, and social spectrum was fed in for scrutiny. The computer replied that the thieves would likely strike the Union National Bank of Danbury, Connecticut, between September 4th and 10th. Then it hedged and recommended light surveillance of certain banks in Ridgefield, Connecticut, and North Salem, New York, over the same period. The computer rejected, on the basis of data from other, solved, robberies, the information that eight men had been involved, setting the number at four.

Carmine Pasarelli was being driven to Waterbury to meet with a fellow capo and ask permission to work his men in another family's territory. In the back seat with him was Lou Katz, his accountant and general manager, who acted on what Carmine thought. "I figure four men, no more than five," Carmine mused. "Guys with houses, cars. Needed cash because of this rotten depression, and boosted a bank. They make about ten grand apiece. They already got clothes, cars, no need to spend money on those. They don't travel it's summer and they got houses in the country, near the beach. They won't be broke till late August, then they start thinkin' money again. They'll make a hit early September, prolly Friday 'cause they hit fine last time on Friday. That piece a cake bank in Danbury we woulda hit if it wasn't in a goombah's territory." Carmine yawned, started to doze. "Send in Inch and Shark. Shoot 'em comin' out." Katz nodded, watched the road.

Schweitzer and Pasarelli helped each other along by involuntary exchanges of information. Carmine's office was bugged and his phone tapped (which he knew), and Schweitzer's men could piece together from random scraps what the family might do next. On the other hand, Carmine's informers told him what the "insurance men" were doing and where, so he had always a good idea what the FBI was up to. In the exchange, the Bureau learned most. When Carmine first heard of the robbery, he was a very angry capo, and in his anger he identified a lieutenant of his organization, one Vito Donatelli of Westport. Donatelli was a genuine find for the Bureau, and identifying him repaid years of futile monitoring of Pasarelli's offices and phones.

Money cannot be permitted to disappear. It may be misappropriated, malused, squandered, loaned, burned, or eaten, but it cannot disappear or society lurches and anarchy looms. A great web forms to entrap it; a noose of many strands is woven about those responsible for its disappearance. One strand was a report by Virgil Overwear, an investigator in the employ of Corporate Fidelity, Inc., the bonding firm. He discovered during a check on (bonded) Malcolm Hayden that Hayden had been elected to membership in the Southport Country Club, a remarkable step up for so ordinary a man. Overwear discovered that while Hayden had been put up for membership by John J. Carmody of Westport, that was only procedure, as Carmody was on the membership committee. Hayden's sponsor had actually been Sanford Campbell of New Canaan. (He learned this from Meyer, the Club steward, who did not approve of Hayden.) No business or social connection between Hayden and Campbell could be discerned. Overwear's information, together with a financial report on Hayden (a $46,000 Tudor ranch in a high tax area on $13,500 a year) was directed to Thomas Clarke, Acting President of The County Trust Company. Clarke had always thought it unusual that Hayden had been invited into the Southport Club, and he called Hayden on it at once. "What's between you and this fella Campbell," he demanded rudely.

"Strictly a banking relationship," Hayden said. "Confidential."

"Not any more it isn't," Clarke told him.

"Between us?"

"How do you know Campbell!" Clarke was not having niceties.

"Between us, he comes in here to cash his unemployment check."

"Unem*ploy*ment check! Are you crazy? The guy's president of a holding company. Four Talents. . . . Oh. I see. Well, I'll be damned. He's collecting unemployment, is he?"

"He *was*," Hayden said. "I don't know if he still is. He hasn't been in here with his check lately."

"And when you asked him to put you up for that Club, he was very agreeable, is that it?" Clarke used only the softest irony.

"Well yes, he was," Mal said. "But I don't think it had anything to do with his unemployment. . . ."

"Good for you." Clarke laughed frankly. "Stay that way. How's business down there?"

"Fantastic," Mal said, and they talked business.

A web. Every Sunday at noon Vito Donatelli found a new pay phone and called the Fortuna Produce Company of Yonkers and asked for Averell, saying he was Harriman. It meant Vito was reporting to Papa Carmine. On Sunday June 8th Papa was so mad he rattled Vito's phone booth, seventeen miles away, and possibly blew the earphones off the cop who monitored the Fortuna Produce lines. Papa wanted to know about anybody in or around Westport, Vito's territory, who suddenly had money, and Papa wanted to know them very, very bad. Vito said he would look around and call back, and he did, with names, but he did not name Jack Carmody, although Jack obviously had sudden money, out of loyalty to a friend. Neither did he tell Jack, after a later visit with Papa Carmine in the South Village, to stay out of Danbury and its bank, out of loyalty to the family. If Jack were guilty, Papa (Inch and Shark) would get him; if he were not guilty, he would not go armed into the Danbury bank. Thus Vito balanced his loyalties effortlessly, simply by shutting his mouth, and he had been raised to prize silence. Every Sunday noon Vito gave Papa the names of people in his territory who had always had money anyway, and were none of them, like Jack Carmody, screwy enough to boost a bank.

Samuel B. Deitsch, d/b/a Miss Svelte, Inc., a subsidiary of Four Talents, Ltd., showed a line of holiday clothes and cruise- and resort-wear in mid-August to establish some accounts receivable and to let the buyers know Sam was still in business. Orders were excellent, but payment would not come until November, after delivery, and possibly later, the economy being what it was.

Betsy Price, née Cameron and a star under that name, was lured from transitory retirement by Jack Carmody to tape a series of bath-oil commercials for the Christmas season. Betsy agreed because her residual income was withering, and she had given her last ten grand to her husband. Besides, she liked being naked. The agency paid cost-plus-fee, but the real money would not come in until after the commercials had been shown, which meant late December or after the first of the year.

The report from the Coast was as follows: *Hargate's Daughters* had grossed a minimum of $4,300,000—according to Immelman & Kurnitz, conservative and respected CPA's. Sid Kransky counterclaimed the picture had grossed only $2,000,000 and had cost $2,100,000 to make, so there was no net gross. Harry Price submitted his books, which showed the picture cost $900,000 to make. Thus Hallowell, Shaw, Embry & Carstairs, Harry's lawyers, were suing Allied Universal productions (Sid Kransky) for $425,000 in one suit and $275,000 in a second suit, plus $200,000 in punitive action. They expected to win less than the most but more than the least. However, the case could not be heard until mid-September, and even with a judgment, collecting money from Kransky might take a long time.

In short, business was good and bankruptcy loomed. (These things take *time*.) Money was going out at an unhealthy rate. Sandy announced that beginning September 1 and until further notice, all draws were to be halved to five hundred a month, and the Company could no longer pay Club bills for the staff. Joanna Deitsch, hearing of this austerity move, called Jack Carmody and asked for some of his private time. Out of manners and curiosity, Carmody acceded.

"I came here to beg for Sam," Joanna began. "You men are broke again now, for a while at least. You're not going to stay broke and you know it. You robbed a bank once, and it was easy, so let's face it, rather then be broke you're going to rob a bank again, right?"

"We might develop other sources of money, Joanna," Carmody said. They were in his den. It was morning and they drank coffee.

"I hope so. Oh, I hope so," Joanna said. "You don't know what that man went through last time. Sleepless, tossing and turning at night, crying out in his sleep, keeping it all inside. Eating his heart out."

"We are none of us professional criminals, Joanna. It hurt all around. But I wouldn't worry about next time."

Joanna surged her generous bottom on the couch. "That's why I'm here, Jack. Jack. Next time let me go with you. Let me take Sam's place and be driver or something. For Sam's sake. You're his friend. Don't put him through that horror again."

Everybody wants to be wheelman, Carmody thought. *Everybody wants to* almost *rob a bank.* He smiled. "Did you have any special bank in mind, Joanna?"

"Yes. Exactly the place. In Danbury. I pass it every Wednesday when I take the kids to visit my parents." Joanna's fists and eyes squinched shut in an ecstasy of cunning. "There's never anybody there, always nobody. Empty. Union National in Danbury." She sighed and relaxed her fists and eyes and smiled.

"I'd have to take this up with the other men, Joanna. I'm not alone in this, you know."

Then Joanna spoke at length and Carmody, in his impatience, overheard roughly thus: "You are Irish gunman insensitive drunk. Sam is Jewish sweet vulnerable family sober. I have nothing to do all day but chauffeur and make sandwiches and I would think it a model orgy to knock over this cute little isolated bank I've found in Danbury. Besides I can drive like the wind and will even steal the car." Actually Joanna spoke for several minutes, perhaps eight.

Her message, in its occasional penetrations and in its gross misunderstandings, irritated Carmody thoroughly. There was also a laziness in him, and there was too much to explain to too little purpose. "If it turns out we need you, Joanna, I know where to find you."

"But you're the *leader!* You can *say!* Once they decide to go in, *you* run things!" She shuddered in massive martyrdom, then bit her lip in a showbiz passion for control.

The gesture annoyed Carmody further. "Well, okay, Joanna," he said, rising. "I'll definitely keep you in mind if we plan anything."

"I won't let Sam *go!* I won't let him go! It's me or nothing!" Joanna stood so suddenly as to seem stung where intimacy occurs. She stomped to the hallway. "Just because I'm not a man you think I'm not steady enough to be driver!"

"Joanna, I appreciate your feelings for Sam, and I share them, but as yet we haven't—"

"You're not getting *my* husband!" Joanna cried, and she banged down the hall to the kitchen and out the back door.

When Joanna was gone, and her car could be heard dangerously racing off, Carmody said aloud to the den: "Drunken Irish gunman. I've gotta do something about my image."

Agents Batista and O'Rourke (a female of Mediterranean aspect although certifiably American in origin) rented the second floor of a frame tenement across Route 7 from the Union National Bank of Danbury. They introduced so much bizarre matériel into the flat that they were compelled against procedure, and on a vow of his secrecy, to reveal themselves to the landlord as FBI operatives. Thereafter friends of the landlord drove by on sunny afternoons to rubberneck the second floor windows, where the telescopes were said to be.

At the same time, across the street, the Union National was being equipped with motion picture, still, and television cameras; with open telephone lines to FBI Stamford (with of course relays to Chevy Chase), and to the Bureau of Motor Vehicles in Hartford. The floor was sprayed nightly with radioactive wax. The bank was staffed with cleancut, well groomed, armed men and women. Similar though less extensive precautions were being taken in neighboring banks in Ridgefield and North Salem.

Beginning August 10, every man, woman, and child who entered the Union National Bank was telescanned, and the image was relayed through Stamford to Chevy Chase. Information on every entering body—bank data, police record, service record, employment history, automobile license and registration, marital status, security clearance, credit rating, political affiliation—was fed into the computer to match images already stored. By August 25th, everyone with regular legitimate business in the bank was identified in Maryland, and the computer turned on a small red light in Danbury when a new image was scanned. The light identified several distressed executives come to cash new unemployment checks, and some superior housewives come to cash welfare checks. One conviction was obtained for welfare fraud and forgery, and a fugitive abortionist from Salt Lake City was identified endorsing travelers' checks and turned over to the Utah police. Thereafter the light rarely lit up, as even irregular visitors became known to the computer.

Exterior surveillance of the bank was conducted from the second floor of the tenement across the highway. Automobile license plate numbers were observed from there and telephoned at once to Motor Vehicles in Hartford for identification.

On the afternoon of Wednesday, September 5th, tensions were building among the agent-bank-staff. If you watch hard enough, long enough—as soldiers know—sooner or later you will see something, whether it is there or not. When a dark woman with a lovely daughter in tow entered the bank, and the red light went on, the agents thought they saw something, whether or not it was there. "I wonder, miss," the dark lady said to the first teller (Agent Harmon), "if my daughter might use your ladies' room. There don't seem to be any decent facilities in the neighborhood."

"Certainly," the teller said, smiling welcome and pressing a button. She led Joanna and Lisa to a small, clean washroom labeled LADIES and left them there. Lisa was viewed live, and also taped, sitting on the john with her slacks still on. Her mother was viewed nosing uselessly around the hallway and the small offices off it. After all the weeks of watching and waiting, the FBI over-reacted, and Operation Rage was set in motion.

The D'Amato brothers, Inch and Shark, fought with such insensate savagery as children that nobody, not even in Yonkers, would fight with them, and they had to be content beating up one another. Ferocity, like other forms of insanity, is of little worth unless channeled and governed, and Carmine Pasarelli directed the D'Amato brothers' insanity to his own ends and in his own fashion. He mastered them by ignoring them generally, abusing them tirelessly when he summoned them, paying them poorly even by hard-guy standards (which are astonishingly low), ragging them, bullying them, spitting on them, then sending them off to face danger. Inch and Shark therefore loved Papa Carmine, and pursued their rare and violent missions in almost comic dread of his wrath. The D'Amatos were sent to hang/gout near the Union National Bank of Danbury, and to burn anybody who came out of it with a gun. Papa directed them, with lavish obscenity, to be especially alert late in the week, early in September.

The Quarterly Report from Four Talents, Ltd., was a modestly handsome four-page photo-offset document describing the organization and its purposes, the activities of its divisions, and the prospects for the coming year. It had a growth chart and a bar graph. It folded in three and had been circulated by mail to the principals of the firm. Viewed sharply, a printed Quarterly Report for Four Talents was an expensive piece of folly.

Because he sensed a turning point in the tide of affairs, Sandy Campbell set up a luncheon meeting in the Haig Room of the Southport Country Club for Wednesday, September 5. He wanted each of the principals to discuss the progress of his division, and to answer the questions of the others, so everybody would know what everybody else was doing. He also wanted an open discussion on financing—that is, how much money they needed for how long, and how best to lay hands on it.

The second business lunch was very different from the first, which had launched the whole project. It was also very different from other gatherings of the four, which in their abandon had been more like reunions of the Vista Bank Veterans Association. The second business lunch was exactly that, a luncheon meeting of four men embarked together on a business venture. At the table, over drinks, Sandy handed around fresh copies of the Quarterly Report. "I assume you've all had a chance to read this," he said. Carmody, Deitsch, and Price opened copies of the Report and read idly.

"How much did this cost?" Carmody asked.

"Three-fifty. But I paid for it out of pocket," Sandy said.

"You shouldn't have done that," Carmody said.

"No," said Sam. "This is a legitimate business expense. Congratulations. It's very stylish."

"Thank you."

"Take it out of company money, Sandy," Price said. "We should all be paying for this kind of thing."

"How many copies did you have run off?" Carmody asked.

"Two hundred. It only cost a couple of bucks more for an extra hundred."

"Good."

It was agreed with vigor that the Company should absorb the cost of the Report. It was worth three-fifty and more to every one of them. In its pedestrian, unremarkable, and altogether business-like way, the Report legitimized an endeavor of illicit beginnings, and lent a minor but definite identity to men who had been in danger of becoming invisible. They were no longer men who "used to be" somebody. They were something and somebody now, right there in black and white. Everybody was pleased that there were at least two hundred copies.

Sandy opened business talk over the second drink, establishing pretty much what everybody knew. Then Harry Price told the story of his lawsuits in California and of an original screenplay he had been writing that they might think of producing next year. Sam Deitsch reported that Miss Svelte, Inc., would be self-supporting after the winter showing of the spring line, and should make good money in the spring. Over steaks, Carmody told of the progress of Harry Price Productions, and confidently predicted sizable profits around the first of the year. It was an informative meeting all around, but more important it established a feeling of mutuality, of common goals reached by group effort. They became more deeply aware that they were dependent on one another, and that if each man held up his end, they would prosper together in a year.

"Which brings us, unfortunately, to the subject of operating capital," Sandy said over coffee. "Cash money now or sooner."

There was a breathless silence; plates were heard to rattle in the kitchen. "We have to figure out how much we need and how badly we need it. The money is there, of course, but there are risks involved. Whenever you take money there is some risk. . . ."

"I can take a mortgage on my house," Sam said. "I was going to anyway, to finance my spring line."

"Thanks, Sam, but I don't think that'll be necessary," Sandy said. "There are other ways to get money." The waiter came out with fresh coffee. Sandy put his thumb to his lips and they all fell silent while the waiter poured. "I've been over the mechanics of this thing with Jack," Sandy said when the waiter was gone, "and Jack agrees, I think. Don't you?" Carmody nodded glumly. "What we've got to do now, just to tide us over this dry spell, is go public."

"What?" Sam shouted.

"Shhh," Sandy said. "The staff here can't be trusted." He lowered his voice and continued. "Now I can't tell you how reluctant I am to surrender even a small percentage of our holdings, but we need money now and we need it badly, so there isn't any choice that I can see. Can you, Jack?"

"No," Carmody said. "I don't like it at all, but we've gotta do it."

"But we don't have any assets," Harry said. "It's outright theft."

"No, it isn't!" Sandy became hotly defensive. "Our accounts receivable are *very* good. They're excellent, as a matter of fact. Besides, the men we'd encourage to invest are men who can afford a small risk. Men like Sinclair, Magruder, Hibbard."

"I hate to surrender any part of it, especially now," Harry said. "All the dirty work is done and we're about to make some real money. . . ."

"But we need *cash*, Harry," Carmody said. "And I don't see any other way. What do you think, Sam?"

"Oh," Sam said. "My God. Sell anything you want. I thought we were going to rob another bank."

"Shush!" they yelled at him. "Rob another bank? Are you crazy?" Sandy whispered hoarsely. They all looked at Sam as though he had been caught in a motel with a sheep.

Exhorting his troops, Papa Carmine had said, in part and translated here roughly from the Napolitano original, "For the sake of your gonorrheal mother's milk-white eyes and the sharp horns on your father's face, fail me not, or there will be a wet cube from the automobile press that will forever smell of D'Amato." Thus cowed, and determined to come back with their shields or on them, Shark and Inch D'Amato sat, on a Wednesday afternoon in early September, in twin Avis rentals in the lot before the Union National Bank of Danbury. They had been sitting in the lot for two days and were bored silly. The bank did little business, and there weren't enough comings and goings to keep them awake. They had revolvers and knives, and Shark had a grenade. He looked up, Shark did, and indicated by ever so faint a nod that Inch was to drive around (again) and check the area for cops. Inch shook his head ever so faintly No, although he would lose if they got to fighting since Shark had the only grenade, tipping the slender balance. When Shark made his kill face, Inch pointed to a pair entering the bank—a dark woman with a girl of infinite grace in tow. Shark nodded, appeased.

With nothing else to do, Agent O'Rourke took to watching the two new agents who had been staked out in the parking lot since Monday. Something was wrong with them, something amiss, but she could not isolate it. They did not look Bureau. Not simply because they were dark and savage-looking and without neckties, but because something was missing, something Bureau men would have, or do. Mrs. O'Rourke could not isolate it. A large red station wagon pulled into the parking lot and a dark woman and a girl-child got out and started for the bank. Agent O'Rourke put off recording the station wagon license number until she had identified what troubled her about the D'Amato brothers.

Joanna Deitsch took Lisa by the hand and led her into the

Union National Bank. The red light went on. A gracious teller took them to a ladies' room, since the child was distressed. When Lisa was telescanned sitting on the john with her slacks on, with her mother outside nosing senselessly around the hall, Agent Schweitzer, bored very nearly to death by the interminable and fruitless bank watch overreacted. He summoned outside agents to come at once, for firepower. Two telephone linemen in full rig and two workmen in coveralls went quickly to the bank. Inch pointed them out to Shark. Shark nodded. It was time. They got out of their Avises. Shark loosened the bandaid on the grenade, the pin having been removed. They closed on the bank. Kill them when they come out. Papa Carmine will be glad.

Nothing is simultaneous, not even light, and just before the D'Amatos got out of their cars, Agent O'Rourke discovered what was wrong with them, why they were not Bureau. The two dark stake-out agents had no babyshoes hanging from their rearview mirrors. "Batista! Batista!" she cried, calling her partner. "Stakeout guineas with no babyshoes!"

"Impossible!" Batista roared, running to look. "No babyshoes? Let me see!" He looked through the telescope and, perhaps not trusting his vision, through the open Itex lens of the Polaroid. "JesusGod! You're right. No babyshoes! They're not *Bureau!*" He picked up a small microphone. "Rage One, Rage One. This is Rage Two, over!"

Shark and Inch took up wide posts on either side of the bank. Their guns were in their hands, ready to cut down the linemen and workmen when they came out. Shark ripped the bandaid from the grenade with his teeth. The handle popped free, spinning bright, end-over-end in the afternoon sun. Shark looked at the grenade in his hand.

"Rage Two, *this* is Rage One, over," Schweitzer said.

"Rage One, this *is* Rage Two!" Batista shouted. "Two armed alleged assailants are engaging your initial front aperture device. Anticipate firefight. Over."

Shark threw the grenade as he had seen them thrown in movies, with a full rotation of his arm. It bounced on the hood of his Avis, the clang loud in the afternoon. Then, with a ferocity impossible to predict or describe, it turned into flame, heat, noise, and flying fragments. The car folded like a beercan. The bank windows flew inward.

"Red Rage! Red Rage!" Schweitzer yelled in a kind of angry joy. The waiting was over. "Red Rage! Red Rage!" The bank immediately became a fortress. Clean-cut, well dressed men and women brandished handguns. Bulletproof glass clanked up before the tellers' cages.

Lisa dried her hands and stepped out into the hallway. Joanna, having found nothing but small empty offices, led her daughter brusquely up the hall. "What the hell are you doing here?" a large blond Nazi man demanded. "Get in the back and under cover!" he ordered. "FBI!" he added. Joanna and Lisa scurried back up the hall to an office and ducked behind a desk. There was a tremendous, sharp explosion out front, a shattering CRACK! and the sound of glass collapsing. Then shots. Bang. Bang-bang. Bang-bang-bang. Loud voices were heard in intolerable obscenities. A horrible ugly fight was in progress. which surprised Joanna, because the bank didn't look Irish.

Then there was peace. Not silence—indeed, there was wild confusion—but peace. Joanna and Lisa went timidly up the hall and unnoticed crossed the large, open banking area. Two savage-looking Sicilians or something sat handcuffed on the bank floor, blood all over their faces. They were swearing at each other. The nice teller who had taken Lisa to the ladies' room stood over them with an enormous black gun in her slender, manicured hand. Joanna and Lisa walked out of the bank to the station wagon and got in. Joanna drove out of the parking lot and north, toward grandmother's house to show off Lisa. "I tell you one thing, young lady, and trust me on this," she said. "Never bank in Connecticut. It's too dangerous."

"Especially on Wednesdays!" Lisa said, and began to laugh

very, very hard, stamping her radioactive foot in delight.

"Right!" Joanna said dubiously, and started laughing, too, although she had not been joking.

"We done it," Inch said. "Him and me. Right, Shark?" The Shark nodded vigorously. The D'Amatos had been beaten, and bled freely from the brows, but it somehow became them.

"Well, of *course* you didn't rob the Vista bank!" Agent Schweitzer howled. "You're too stupid! You're muscle! Thugs! Hard-guys! You couldn't plan a handjob!"

"We done it, all right," Shark said. Inch nodded, hard. They were assembled in the almost antiseptic conference room of the Danbury jail—Shark and Inch, Schweitzer, two former telephone linemen, and a former bank clerk. "Get them outta here!" Schweitzer bawled, pointing at the D'Amatos. "OutOutOut! Send them back to Papa Carmine."

"You kraut Nazi pig!" Inch spat. "You can't. We're guilty!"

"Out!" Schweitzer yelled.

The D'Amatos stood. "Just a minute, Mister Smartass FBI," Shark said. "I know my rights! I say I knocked over the Vista bank, you gotta hold me!"

"He's right!" Inch cried. "Besides, we're wanted in California for a thing we did. Extra*dit*ion, I think it was." Inch thought a spell. "Maybe you could arrange that?'

"Not a chance," Schweitzer said evenly. "I'm sending you back to Papa. Out! Out!" Agents herded the D'Amatos toward the door.

"We was armed!" Shark cried.

"You have licenses, may God have mercy on somebody's soul," Schweitzer said.

"But I had a grenade!" Shark cried, inspired. "You *gotta* hold me for that!"

"I'm releasing you under the War Souvenirs Act," Schweitzer said, and smiled savagely.

"Oh." They stood, shoulders touching, the two most vicious

kids in the history of Yonkers, which is to say the world, in the antiseptic doorway. "We got our rights," Inch said hopelessly. "We cop a plea guilty you gotta arrest us."

"Back to Papa."

"Charlie FBI," Shark said reasonably. "You know you're one crazy mean sonofabitch?"

"Back to Papa."

Shark and Inch, unmanacled, walked through the open door toward frightful liberty.

"I'll have stock shares printed," Sandy said. "Nothing gaudy, but on good paper." It was two o'clock in the Haig Room. "And I'll have Price, Waterhouse do an audit on our first quarter. They don't need to know where the seed money came from. I thought of having a good house—Smith, Barney, for example—float the issue, but we're small for that yet. We can do the selling ourselves, to friends who can afford a small risk. After all, one of our greatest assets is having a lot of friends who can afford a small risk.

"Anyway, I think that wraps it, gentlemen. Any questions or contributions?" There were none. Sandy stood. "I know it's just after two, but I think we might celebrate our going public with some of Mister Carmody's famous stingers, and get down to the nitty-gritty tomorrow. Jack?"

"I'd be glad to make them," Carmody said, "but I'm not doing any serious drinking until after six these days."

"I have a meeting on the Coast tonight," Harry Price said. "I'll be punchy enough after the flight."

"Not for me," Sam said. "I need my head. I have to see the union this afternoon. You drink for me, Sandy."

"Oh, not alone," Sandy said.

Everybody shook hands with everybody else, and they went their separate businesslike ways. Wherever events had briefly taken them, they were, for better or worse, home again now.